All Bitter and Twisted

by

Ron Bennett MBE

First published in 2004

PUBLISHED BY
PAUL MOULD PUBLISHING UK

IN ASSOCIATION WITH
EMPIRE PUBLISHING SERVICES USA

ISBN 1-904959-11-3

Printed in Great Britain by
CLE Print Limited

Dedication

This book is dedicated to my wife Christine who, like all Forces wives, endures the rigors of Service life with little recognition and without any reward. Thank you my Angel.

CHAPTER 1

A thick soup of fog rolled across the flat Lincolnshire fens swallowing everything in its path. By dawn the fog had become so dense that every sound seemed to have been suppressed. An ominous silence had descended upon the little bit of MOD real estate that Corporal Ben Brownley had been detailed to guard.

Ben Brownley was a stocky, powerfully built, 28-year-old Welshman. He stood alone. His teeth chattered and his muscular body shivered inside the next to useless cold weather protective clothing, with which he had been issued. His very soul seemed to be numbed to the core as the air temperature had plummeted to minus 5. The flat, windswept fenlands could be a very inhospitable location at the best of times. Alone on exercise guard early that autumn morning in 1999 was definitely one of those times. A huge iridescent dew-drop disengaged itself from his red, raw nose. It fell earthwards to splatter onto the toe cap of one of his mud-encrusted combat boots.

The sun struggled in vain to make an overdue appearance through the opaque fog and morning mist. Brownley fingered the pistol grip of his SA80 with a gloved hand. He was conscious that he had removed and replaced, for the umpteenth time on that guard stint, his empty magazine. This was in a vain attempt to stave of a severe attack of boredom. At least when blank ammunition was issued, he thought to himself, it added some semblance of realism to the task in hand. But for some reason, most probably financial, no blanks had been issued on this exercise. His inner-most thoughts contented him to the fact that at least his arctic combat gloves kept his digital extremities warm. They had been given to him by an old school mate who was now in 3 Para. Ben Brownley had been told that the secret to arctic survival was to keep hand and especially the wrist warm, as they are the thermostats of the body. These gloves were his prized possession and were well worth the crate of beer he had swapped them for.

Gazing to his front into the grey infinity; he contemplated his lot. He mused to himself, by trying to recall the impressive sales pitch from the bullshitting Sergeant at the Careers Information Office. Brownley was sure that this not so glamorous side of Air Force life was definitely not mentioned those eight long years ago. He'd convinced himself that by now he should have been sunning himself on a beach in Cyprus or swapping spit with some dusky maiden in some other exotic part of the world. Instead he was guarding, or at least pretending to guard, an aviation fuel installation at the southern eastern corner of the airfield at Royal Air Force Hemingsby. He was guarding it from an imaginary enemy that would probably be a Rock Ape or RAF Regiment Infantryman to give him his formal title. Rock Ape was the nickname long associated with the RAF Regiment. Nobody knew were it came from but it was one of the numerous nicknames given to the many trades or units within the Services, the origin of most where lost in the mists of time. Rock Apes got a kick out of charging around airfields, blasting off hundreds of rounds of blank ammunition, slinging thunderflashes and smoke grenades around like demented pyromaniacs and generally causing chaos and grief to the poor, lowly, groundcrew 'grunts'.

The Station often brought in the Regiment to act as enemy on exercises. They were supposed to play the game within the rules of the exercise. What usually happened was they'd run amok everywhere on the station, pissing off all the friendly forces and generally having a great big hoot. It was expected to help sharpen their infantry skills. It more likely sharpened their wit and twisted their warped sense of humour even further.

The low lying, ice-laden fog had cut visibility down to less than 10 yards. Brownley could just make out each end of the grassy-banked fuel bunker he has been detailed to guard. To his front lay the double rolls of frost-encrusted barbed wire that spiralled off to both left and right, disappearing into the mist. It had been a couple of hours since the guard commander had posted him on Bulk Aviation Fuel Installation - Number 6. He had said he would be back with a replacement within two hours.

" So were the bloody hell was he?" Brownley thought to himself, "Typical! Us poor soddin' canon-fodder left stuck out guarding a poxy fuel bunker, that's more than likely empty anyway." He knew that no self respecting terrorist or special forces soldier would have been seen dead trying to take out a place like this, when there was more important targets like aircraft or aircrew around.

Brownley, fed up with waiting, reached for the land-line telephone to call up the guard control post. Suddenly a deafening explosion rang out from beyond the fuel bunker's grassy embankment. He instantly recognized that it came from a 'thunderflash', which was a large, noisy firework type of device used to simulate explosions. Spinning round, Brownley was startled to see two armed Rock Apes bearing down on to him from the top of the banking. They both had weapons with a yellow blank ammunition firing attachment fitted to the barrel of their rifles. These devices were fitted for safety and permitted the rifle to automatically reload a blank round once one had been expended. Brownley knew they would not open fire being so close to the fuel installation; that was the rule for exercise play. So he was rocked back on his heals as both assailants rattled of several rounds aimed straight at him. A blur of green and brown camouflage uniform rushed onto his position. They exaggerated their war-like look by baring their teeth, which contrasted against the dark streaks of their camouflaged faces. Brownley had, for some unknown reason, focused his vision onto the sole of one of the black combat boots worn by the lead attacker as it descending from above, straight at him. Its image seemed to fill the whole of his field of view. It appeared to be moving in agonizingly slow motion towards him. The distinctive sole pattern registered in Brownley's mind because it matched the multitude of footprints that lay all around the guard post he had occupied for the past two hours or so. Both attackers charged down the steep bank. They both landed a few feet from were Brownley stood. Before he could bring his weapon to bear on the intruders or raise the alarm, a bone crunching shoulder charge was skillfully applied to Brownley's chest by the lead attacker. Bowled over backwards by the impact, all the air in his lungs was instantly expelled. It was far more effective than any tackle that Brownley had ever experienced during the many years he had been playing rugby.

As his senses started to return, Brownley found himself lying on the cold, frost- hardened ground. He was immediately struck by a strong pungent smell of damp sacking which was saturating his nostrils. A lattice of light permeated the sandbag hood that engulfed his head and his hands were bound firmly together behind his back.

"Tagged and bagged," he muttered to himself, "The classic calling card of pseudo-special forces. Those miserable pissing Rock Apes must have loved this, hooding and tying up a penguin." A penguin, of course, was their term of endearment for groundcrew. In the eyes of the RAF Regiments, all groundcrew were - 'all flap and no fly!'

But there wasn't a sound from them anywhere around where Brownley lay. What he could hear by now was the easily recognizable sound of a Landrover approaching. "This must be the guard commander at last," he thought to himself.

Sergeant Chris Liversidge was a plump, cheery Yorkshireman and was the guard commander for that sector of the airfield. He was a good guy and was well liked by all the lads. He worked everyone hard but was fair and he was known for looking after his troops when it was needed. Chris jumped out of the Landrover, ran across and ripped off the sand bag that covered Brownley's head. It was obvious he was not amused, Brownley could tell by the tone of his voice, when he said:

"You stupid prat, Ben! What the hell have you been up to? I hope you realize that the Boss is livid. You've let those 'rocks' take out the only fuel bunker left on the exercise. He'll be having your guts for this you know!"

Colin helped Ben to his feet as he pointed to the large day-glo sticker, which was now attached to the main delivery valve of the fuel bunker. It declared the fuel installation had, for the purposes of the exercise, been destroyed courtesy of 47 Squadron RAF Regiment. Brownley was more than a little taken aback. He knew he'd really screwed up and was due for a bollocking of biblical proportions from the Boss.

But, as Brownley moved towards the Landrover, he suddenly noticed his weapon was missing. He looked anxious as he scanned the immediate area for the personal weapon that he'd signed for. Sgt Liversidge suddenly realized the young corporal's dilemma and spoke tersely to Brownley,

" Just don't tell me you have lost your bloody weapon as well...because if you have, your feet won't touch the ground when Burton gets hold of you." Brownley resigned himself to his gloomy fate and climbed into the back of the Landrover and sat down. He hung his head between his knees, clasped his hands behind his head and expelled a sigh that said it all.

The 'Boss' was not only Brownley's exercise commander but Flight Lieutenant Julian Burton was also the Junior Engineering Officer, in RAF parlance, the Jengo. He commanded the Aircraft Maintenance Flight, AMF for short, which was where Brownley worked. Burton was not the most well-liked or respected member of the flight. It could have been expected by most that, as an ex-ranker, he would have been a little more sympathetic to the plight of the lower ranks. But not bloody likely! Ever since he'd arrived, he'd rapidly evolved into a right autocratic bastard and everyone agreed that he seemed to be getting worse. One of the airframe technicians in Hydraulic Bay had told Brownley that he had been on a Jaguar squadron in Germany several years ago with Burton, when he was a fresh-faced corporal electrician. Even then he was widely known as a bit of a plonker. Another case of a self-opinionated tosser who realized that he wasn't good enough to make Sergeant, so he took the easy way out and opted instead for a commission. This resulted in a trip to Cranwell for the full lobotomy, which was compulsory; the spine removal, of course, was optional. Burton had both and was duly commissioned and turned out on the big wide Air Force as one of Lord Trenchard's finest. Unfortunately Brownley was saddled with him as his flight commander. For some strange reason, which totally escaped the comprehension of most people, the upper management loved him. So Brownley braced himself for the bollocking, which even by his own admission, he richly deserved. To let the enemy get one over you is one thing, but losing a rifle - is suicidal.

The Station tannoy burst into life just above Brownley's head, as he ambled down the corridor leading to the Jengo's office. It announced that the exercise was now terminated and all personnel were to return weapons back to the Armoury and commence the post exercise clean-up. Brownley knew that his weapon would find its way back eventually. At that moment in time he didn't care anyway. Outside Flt Lt Burton's office door Ben Brownley tried to tidy himself up a bit. Straightening his beret and buttoning up jacket pockets, he rubbed his toe caps up the back of his trouser legs in a vain attempt to add a bit of a shine to his well worn, muddy boots. Brownley rapped on the office door in fine military fashion and awaited a summons.

Brownley stood for what seemed likes hours, awaiting an invitation to be issued with the latest of his numerous bollockings for the year. He heard nothing. Brownley rapped again on the door. Still no answer. He turned the doorknob and poked his head inside Burton's lair. Flt Lt Burton was seated at his desk and was talking on the phone. Judging by the tone of his smarmy, subservient voice he was talking to the squadron commander, the Senior Engineering Officer - the Sengo. Burton's eyes bulged, his eye brows arched and a prominent vein pulsed on his fore head at the sight of his uninvited guest. He cupped the mouth piece with his hand and bellowed at Cpl Brownley,

" Get out! - How dare you enter my office without my permission!" Brownley recoiled back and closed the door as quickly and quietly as he could. He looked skywards, his eyes rolling in their sockets "Oh bloody marvellous," Brownley muttered to himself, "Burton's going to be in a brilliant mood after this."

Brownley knew that had just about kissed good-bye to any promotion prospects that he might have had. He saw in his minds eye his third strip disappearing off over the horizon like a cruise missile. However his depressing contemplations were interrupted by Burton's voice summoning him back into his office. Brownley swallowed hard, straightened his backbone and stepped smartly towards his fate.

Inside the office Burton sat in his chair still dressed in his combats. On exercises most officers were issued with a 9 mm automatic pistol. His was laid on the desk next to the phone. The young Corporal knew he was in the shit and was

8

due a damn good shafting. But he thought not even Burton would shoot him for screwing up on an exercise. Then reality dawned and he remembered that no live ammunition is ever issued for exercises. So his mortal soul was safe...for the moment at least.

Brownley stood rigid to attention in front of the desk. Burton started to rip into his wayward corporal regarding his piss-poor performance during the recently terminated exercise. Brownley suddenly remembered an invaluable tip to adopt when receiving a verbal from a superior officer. This had been passed on to him by one of the instructors way back in basic training. It was one of those golden nuggets of information, absorbed during those first hectic but informative months, that for some strange reason was stored in the memory forever.

His mind wondered back to that instructor. He couldn't remember his name, but he could distinctly remember his words of wisdom. He recalled such wonderful snippets like, "Never volunteer for anything "and "Always get the first word in when meeting the Station Warrant Officer, to fend off the obligatory bollocking you would inevitably receive due to your scruffy appearance." Of course, Ben Brownley knew that everyone was scruffy in the eyes of the SWO. But a cheery "Hello or Good morning, Sir" seemed to work, ...well most of the time.

Brownley fixed his stare, just as the instructor had advised, over the right shoulder and out of the window that stood behind his now, ranting and raving Boss. This helped to deaden the ferocity of the tongue-lashing he was on the receiving end of. He vaguely registered words like 'promotion prospects' and 'incompetence', which emerged above the general melee of verbosity. Brownley could slowly feel an inner smile hatching, as he remembered that Burton was nearing the end of his two year tour at Hemingsby. He would be off soon to torment somebody else and screw up some other poor sod's career. Brownley knew that he could easily weather any bollocking by just switching off and smiling inward to himself. His stare by-passed the face of his Boss but was now firmly focused on the line of aircraft that could just be seen through the rapidly clearing fog on the dispersal outside the office window. The linies, as they were known, who did all the first line work like refueling, re-oiling and rearming, were swarming all over the recently landed aircraft like soldier ants. Brownley recalled his last posting as a liney with some pleasant affection. That's what he'd joined up to do: the sharp end - dealing with flying aircraft and aircrew.

His current posting in AMF was more technically demanding but was a constant, hard slog; repairing and servicing Tornado aircraft day after day for the flying squadrons but with no chance of the fringe benefits that they had, like the occasional detachment to the sunnier climes in the world. Suddenly a face loomed over Burton's shoulder outside the window. It masked the sight of the frantic activities on the parked aircraft. Brownley recognized the unmistakable and distinctive features of Cpl Dixie Dean grinning wildly like a Cheshire cat.

CHAPTER 2

Dixie and Ben were big muckers. They went back a long way playing rugby together. They formed two thirds of RAF Hemingsby RFC 's front row of the scrum. Dixie had been propping Ben for the past four seasons and the infamous 'front row union' has never seen such a solid allegiance. They played together for the station and a local civvy team. They drank together, fought together, chased the same women together and were generally inseparable.

Ben remembered, with some amusement, the first day he had met Dixie at a 7-a-side rugby tournament over five years ago. In fact he recalled it was at the end of season tournament known, throughout of the Air Force, as the 'Binbroke Bomb Tournament.' Ben had only been at Hemingsby for a couple of months and had arrived late into the rugby season. He was not well known to all the team and a bit of an unknown quantity to the Coach. So he only went with the squad to make up the numbers. He didn't really expect to command a place in the team but the day was guaranteed to be good fun and extremely sociable.

The Hemingsby 'sevens' team was very proficient and were holders of the Binbroke Bomb Trophy at that time. Ben found it a little frustrating to be there but not playing a full part in the competition. There were many players from other units, who were also available but unlikely to play for their respective teams. Not long after arriving at the pitches Ben bumped into a veteran player and coach that he knew, from when he played for the RAF Under 23 side. His name was Flight Sergeant Brian Harshaw, a rugby mad Irishman, who at forty-two was still running round like a teenager. Brian suggested that a scratch team be put together from all the players who couldn't get into their unit's side. They could then enter a side in the Plate Competitions. The Plate Competition ran alongside the main Trophy Competition. It enabled all the teams who were knocked out in the first round, to play at least one more game before retiring into the beer tent.

Nine or ten players had a quick training session under the wise guidance of Brian. They entered the team into the Plate under the auspicious name of the 'Beertent Barbarians.' It took a bit of smooth talking by Brian to bend the rules to allow the team to enter. However in the spirit of free running rugby and a promise of several beers to the adjudicator, their entry was finally accepted.

Ben introduced himself to all the assembled players. There were a couple of players he had met before. These included a tall second row forward called Glyn from RAF Llantwit and a couple of fit looking wingers called Woody and Andy from RAF Feldbruch. The rest of the players, in turn, introduced themselves.

Ben was sat on the grass retying his boots. From behind a loud belch rattled out from the door of the beertent. A few seconds later a pair of muddy boots, which had been repaired several time with black insulation tape, appeared next to him. Ben looked up at the anonymous stout legs, which the feet belonged to. The impressive muscular form of Dixie Dean was grinning down at Ben. His facial expression was only interrupted, when he raised the can of beer to his lips. Dixie spoke in his loud cockney accent,

"What d'yer know. What d'yer say, mate. I'm Dixie Dean, any chance of a game?

Ben smiled and nodded in Brian's direction. Ben knew this larger than life character, that had just offered his services, must have been another front row player. Dixie's legs and shoulders were solid and his hands were like shovels. And his looks would not have any modeling agency beating down the door for his services on the catwalk either. Therefore Ben was in no doubt that Dixie must have been, like him, a forward.

Dixie was draining the last dregs of his beer, when Brian threw a ball at him. Without taking the can from his lips he caught the ball, in mid-flight, with one hand. He smiled at his own impromptu party trick, pitched the ball into the nearby rubbish bin and spun passed the empty beer-can back at Brian.

Ben immediately warmed to his new-found colleague and fellow front row player. He just knew he could play with this guy. They hit it off straight away and were soon talking serious rugby tactics for the imminent game.

The 'Beertent Barbarians' played their first game and despite a bit of a wobbly start they were soon throwing the ball around in the finest traditions of real Barbarian rugby. It would have made the likes of Phil Bennett, Gareth Edwards proud to watch...well maybe!

The team survived up to the quarter finals of the competition. They where finally beaten, very convincingly, by a guest Army team. The rumour rife in the beertent was that the Army team had deliberately lost in the first round. This would automatically enter them in the Plate competition, where lesser sides would probably be weaker opposition. They were a very strong side and it was obvious they were after some silverware to take home. 'Cup hunting' was not well-liked by the rugby fraternity and was definitely against the spirit of the whole days event.

After the Beertent Barbarians were knocked out of the competition, they returned to the real beertent for a spot of refreshment. Dixie stood at the bar and ordered each of the players a beer. He told the barman that Brian Harshaw, who was stood at the back of the crowd around the bar, would pay the bill. As the day evolved into the early evening and then into the night, Ben and Dixie forged a friendship for life.

Dixie chatted to Ben over a beer. He explained that he was working, at that time, at a Maintenance Unit, which repaired a vast array of aircraft electronic components. It was a factory type of environment and he hated it. Ben told his new-found mate that Hemingsby always seemed to be short of manpower and suggested he applied for a posting.

Six months later Dixie turned up at RAF Hemingsby. Dixie was posted into AMF to join Ben. Dixie was a "Fairy" or to be precise, an avionics technician and his job was to fix the radar equipment on the aircraft. Ben, however, was a propulsion specialist or as it was more commonly known within the Service as a "Sooty". This nickname went back many years when all propulsion tradesmen's general appearance was usually dirty, oily and sooty from crawling inside jet-pipes of the engines. Nowadays the aircraft engines were more user-friendly and a damn sight cleaner both inside and out.

Eventually Ben found out that Dixie was not his real name. He'd been christened Andrew. But like many servicemen, he had attracted the time-honored nickname, which was always paired with certain surnames. The usual ones found on any unit were, Dusty Miller, Chalky White and for some inexplicable reason, Tug Wilson. Dixie could, in no way, be described by anyone as an Adonis. His short wiry hair capped a face that really did look like a bag of spanners. Despite this women were attracted to him like bees to a honey pot.

Brownley was still enduring the carpeting by Flt Lt Burton, who was embarking on his final volley of negative pleasantries on the subject of Ben's lack of promotion prospects. Ben was pleased with himself. He had survived the ordeal so far. He had kept his solemn, respectful facial expression right up to the point that Dixie Dean had made his unscheduled appearance at the window. Dixie started to imitate the animated mannerisms of Burton. He suddenly stopped his mimicking and produced an angelic look of innocence on his ugly face. He then made a derogatory gesture with his right hand that normally suggested the recipient was a right wanker. It immediately resulted in a burst of laughter that Brownley almost, but not quite, managed to suppress. That must have been the final straw to Burton, who was unaware of Dixie's presence behind. He bellowed at Brownley to get out and come back when he had learned some manners and respect of his superiors.

Brownley left the office pretty sharpish and sought the sanctuary of the corridor to regain his composure. A few minutes later Dixie sauntered down the corridor. He met Ben with his usual greeting,

"What d'ye know, what d'ye say, Benny Boy?
Brownley told Dixie why he was getting an ear bending from Burton and thanked him, with no small degree of sarcasm, for his contribution towards his early ejection from the proceedings. Dixie shrugged his shoulders and offered to buy Ben a beer or two in the bar later that evening, as a way of an apology. Ben agreed. He could never be annoyed with Dixie for long.

They were stood outside Burton's office door chatting about the game they'd played on the previous Wednesday. A few minutes later Senior Aircraft Woman Chrissy Vines, the squadron clerk, came down the corridor. Still in her combats and clutching a pile of mail and files, she was heading for the Jengo's office. Dixie with his usual devil-may-care approach to chatting up the fairer sex turned his charms in her direction. She brushed aside his clumsy advances, dropped the mail off in Burton's office and left. Burton must have asked her if Brownley was still outside, because a few minutes later he came to the door. In a far less agitated manner he was almost pleasant, when he invited Brownley back into his office. When Burton saw Dixie there as well, he smirked slightly and said to him,

" Ah, Corporal Dean. Another of my least favourite corporals. I need to see you as well. Wait there until I call for you."
Ben glanced at Dixie. Neither of them knew why he wanted to speak to them both or why he was in such an unusually civil mood.

Cpl Brownley stood again at attention in front of Burton's desk. This time he could clearly see his own blue personal file open in front of him Burton quickly skipped over the remainder of the rollicking, which he'd terminated so abruptly earlier on. It was nowhere as bellicose as the first one but the message was still the same. He explained that he thought that Brownley was, without doubt, a complete and utter lost cause. He added that no amount of counselling from him would make the slightest bit of difference to Brownley's woeful performance. Burton's face cracked slightly and an embryo of a smile formed on his lips. The reason for this was obvious when Burton told Brownley that the problem would no longer be his to worry about. The blue personal file, which had just arrived in the mail, contained a posting notice. Brownley was off to RAF Feldbruch in Germany and posted on to a Tornado GR5 squadron. Ben could hardly contain his delight. As Brownley was about to leave the office, Burton fired his parting shot,

"Well, Brownley. You've landed a plumb posting. It looks like the newly forming 701 Squadron. You can be assured that I'll not forget what's happened here today. I can also assure you that it will be reflected in your annual assessment. Which, of course, will ensure your chances of making it into the Sergeants' Mess about as much as a snowball's in hell. Now get out of my office, send in Dean and I hope I never have the misfortune to have you work for me again." The ominous warning past right over Brownley's head as he left the room. His thoughts were clearly miles away. In Germany to be precise.

Brownley was waiting in the corridor for Dixie Dean to re-emerge. While he waited he'd been giving some serious consideration as to which car he would buy when he got out to Feldbruch. Dixie came out of the office after a few minutes with a big beaming smile on his ugly face.

"So what did he want?" Ben asked. Dixie explained that he had also been posted to 701 Squadron at Feldbruch. Ben was delighted with their news. Off to Feldbruch together; 701 were about to get the best propulsion and radar technician the Royal Air Force had to offer. More importantly, Feldbruch Panthers RFC would get a new hooker and prop.

The next day Brownley and Dean were both summoned to the Flight Sergeant's office to receive further details of their postings. Brownley was asked by the Flight Sergeant, if he would go without the usual fifty six days notice for a posting, as manpower was needed immediately to start setting up the squadron's engineering facility. Brownley being single with no ties, agreed to go after the seven days embarkation leave, to which he was entitled. Dixie's trade was not needed so urgently, so he would follow out a month or two later.

Back at his room Ben packed up his kit ready to go on leave back to his brother's house in Wales. He set off for the drive in his battered old Escort. He'd already told Dixie that he could have his car after he'd flown out to Feldbruch. It only had a few months MOT left, so Dixie could drive it into the ground if he wanted. Ben Brownley had his mind on a spanking new car, probably a BMW. It had to be something really flash and a dead-certain fanny magnet.

Ben had done the trip across the country to North Wales many times. The last one was back in January, when he'd gone back to spent New Years Eve at his brother's house and see in 1999.

After both of their parents died when Ben was only six years old, Ben had been brought up by his elder brother Wally. As Wally was married, the local authorities allowed him to become Ben's legal guardian.

Times had been hard. Throughout all of his working life, until it finally closed down only a few years ago, Wally had worked at the huge steel works that towered over the small village of Brymbo, which lay a few miles north of Wrexham in Clwyd. Throughout the turbulent times of the seventies, the unions had dominated and, far too often, disrupted most of the industrial output of the country. The all too familiar wildcat strikes and disputes had justly earned Britain a militant industrial reputation right around the world. Wally had avoided all that. He was proud of the fact that Brymbo Steelworks had never been a closed shop and he'd only lost a few weeks work to industrial action in the whole of the thirty years he had worked there. He was not an active union man although he was a member of the union, like many of the workers at Brymbo Steelworks. A sensible arrangement of discussion and negotiation had existed between all employees and management. This meant strikes were non existent. Everyone got on with the job and kept the wages rolling in. With the extra mouth of Ben to feed this money was essential.

Ben remembered growing up with the constant sight of workers disputes and picketing on the t.v. news almost every day. Right up until the Tories won the election in 1979, the cancer of unionism and militancy had shaped and influenced the thoughts of young Ben. He vowed to Wally, even at that early age, that he would never take a job, which would make him a slave to the unions. The winds of change blew, and the uncontrolled power of the unions was tempered by the Tory Government led by the Iron Lady, Maggie Thatcher. Throughout the Tory reign Wally had worked all the overtime he could to help clothe and feed Ben. He gave whatever free time he did have to take his young brother camping, shooting and fishing. Wally was the father that Ben had never really known.

As Ben reached his teens, he realized the sacrifices Wally and his wife Sarah had made to bring him up. Ben decided then that he would join the Armed Forces as soon as practical. This would give him a career, a home and most of all, help relieve the burden on his big brother. Wally didn't try to dissuade young Ben. He was delighted at the career he'd chosen. He had expected, at one time, that he would have followed their father into the Army. Ben, however, was absolutely fascinated by the aircraft that regularly streaked low overhead heading towards the low flying areas of Snowdonia. During the Gulf War he'd been riveted to the t.v. news every evening. He watched in awe at every event and air battle, as it unfolded. So it was the RAF Careers Information Office that he visited one April's day in 1991.

Ben still was fondly remembering how proud that Wally had been the day he'd passed out of training, when the battered Ford rolled up outside his brother's house. Wally and Sarah were in the garden together and were very pleased to see Ben again after ten months. Wally seemed a little preoccupied at first but he did liven up, when Ben told of his posting overseas.

"This deserves a pint or two," Wally declared. So the two brothers set off on the long walk down the hilly lanes to their local, The Ty Inn.

On the road down to the pub Ben chatted to his brother about his job. Wally admitted he'd found it a little difficult to re-adjust to life away from the steelworks, after the many years he had been there. He had been retrained as a HGV driver but Wally admitted he hated it.

"If you are a young bloke," explained Wally. "And you do the long hauls and continental runs, then the pay's pretty good." Wally was getting on a bit and he admitted that he just didn't want all that. Instead he wanted to be home each evening with his wife. So he opted for all the short runs he could. It was a living, but next to no job satisfaction at all. Ben was certain that his brother was hiding something but, as they had just arrived at the pub car park, Ben left it at that.

The Ty Inn had been the oasis for many years to the thirsty steelworkers, as they knocked off work at the end of their long grueling shift. The landlord was a huge man-mountain, ex-professional wrestler called Ross Evans. He and Wally were good mates and went rough shooting wildfowl and rabbits together whenever they could. Despite the closure of the steelworks, the Ty Inn still managed to provide a reasonable living for Ross and his family. It was an old-fashioned drinkers pub. It still boasted a decent darts team and Ross had banned all of those bloody awful space invader machines and juke boxes.

Ben and Wally sat in the bar and slowly sipped at the wonderful beer that Ross served. There were only a few other people in the bar and the two brothers sat and chatted together. Ben was certain that Wally had something on his mind but he could not fathom out what it was. Wally drained his glass and went off into the toilet. It was Ben's round, so he went to the bar for two more beers. He leaned across the bar and quietly asked Ross what was the problem with his brother. With them being such good mates he thought that Ross might be able to help. The larger-than-life landlord did not offer any ideas but his tone lead Ben to believe he was covering for his pal. Ross had to leave the bar to change the empty barrel of bitter. Two big gorilla-like blokes with tattoos and extremely short-cropped hair stood up together from their table near the bar. They went into the toilet together. A few minutes later they both came out and sat down again. Ben was surprised that they'd come out before his brother. He thought maybe he was ill, so Ben went into the toilet to check on him.

In the toilet, Ben found Wally sprawled out on the floor with blood dripping from his nose. He pushed a hanky over Wally's nose and took him back into the bar. Wally was shaking as he walked. Ben knew something was wrong.

"What the bloody hells' happened, " Ben asked Wally. Wally did not reply. He just stared in the direction of the two Neanderthals. Ben shouted over to them,

"Either of you two arseholes know anything about this," pointing to his brother. Wally nudged Ben and muttered through the hanky,

"Forget it, Ben, it's just a nose bleed."
The two gorillas stood up and walked side by side over towards Ben's table and stood in front of him. One of them growled rather than spoke,

"So what if it was," he pointed at Wally, "he shouldn't be such a scab. So shut the fuck up or you'll get the same."

Ben disengaged himself from his brother and launched himself forward. He drove his head between the two thugs, his powerful arms wrapped around their waists. Gripping their shirts at the back, he twisted his fist and yanked down. He had done this many times on the field, when tackling big beefy forwards. It was normally very effective and it was again. It pulled back the heads of his two assailants as their shirt necks compressed their windpipes. This gave Ben the edge and the power of his drive pushed both the men back across the bar floor. A large oak table stood behind them. It impacted just above the backside of the two men who were now rapidly reversing firmly attached to and propelled by Ben. As the table skidded across the tiled floor of the bar, its stout wooden legs emitted an ear-piercing screech. This stopped abruptly, when the table met the bar wall. The force of Ben's powerful recoil continued and it slammed both his opponent's backs down onto the tabletop. The one on the left groaned and rolled on to the floor with a shuddering thud. The other tried to get up. Ben released his vice-like grip and smashed his forearm onto the inviting, stubbled chin that lay before him. It stunned and stopped the mouthy gorilla from advancing any further.

Suddenly Ben felt the strong arms of Ross pulling him away. It stopped any more contact between the two warring figures. Ross shouted at both of the other men to get out of his pub. Ben was incensed with what had been inflicted on his brother. He yelled after the two thugs, as they scuttled away towards the door of the bar. Globules of spittle shot across the bar in their direction,

"You bastards had better keep away from my brother or I'll fucking have you."

After the excitement had calmed down, Ross's wife took Wally into the back room to clean up his bloody nose. Ross brought Ben a large brandy across to his table. Ben was still shaking after his intervention on his brother's behalf. He asked Ross again what had been going on? Ross realized that he couldn't keep quiet any longer.

He sat back and started to explain what had happened after Wally had been made redundant from the Steelworks. Wally had been devastated, when the works was closed down. He'd drifted into the job of HGV driving. Unfortunately the firm was strictly a union run operation. At first it wasn't a problem. The union didn't have too much power, thanks to strict industrial legislation and regulations, which were the legacy of Mrs. T. However, things started to change...slowly at first. Within two years of Labour's massive landslide election win in 1997, the unions saw the chance to regain some of its pre-Tory power and influence. Despite the promises of no return to the bad old days of militancy, most of the unions in the area had gradually started to exert pressure on its membership and management. The union leaders wanted power and all the trappings that went with it. They gambled on the reluctance of the newly elected Labour Government not to buck the unions and bite the hand that fed them. It seemed to pay off. Union membership grew rapidly. They demanded considerable pay raises and radical changes to their working condition. It seemed crystal clear to the whole country that the unions were on a collision course with the management.

Ben was shocked at what he had heard. How was it possible for Wally to go through this without him knowing? Ross smiled slightly and reminded Ben that his brother was a very proud man and he was determined that the unions wouldn't beat him. He had worked for years without their interference and he didn't need them now. Ross elaborated further,

"It had become a challenge to Wally. He just wouldn't lie down and take any crap from the union thugs. Things came to a head, when the union's conveenors called for a work-to-rule. Of course, Wally wasn't having any of it. He refused to abide by the union directive and stop all overtime. Wally wanted the extra wages and continued to drive his normal hours and drive through pickets. Then one or two heavies were sent by the union to apply a bit of pressure and lean on him". Ross looked straight at Ben as he raised his glass to his lips and drained the remains of his pint.

"How do you think Wally answered them?" Ross inquired of Ben.

" He probably told them to 'eff off, get a life and leave him alone" Ben replied. Ross grinned and added,

" Spot on, lad. Spot on! "

Events didn't stop there. Ross related to Ben what happened after that,

" Wally had taken some bloody awful grief and aggravation from most of the blokes he worked with. Sarah told him to leave and get a job somewhere else. But Wally would not give in and his resistance stiffened even more. His truck got trashed, poor old Sarah got cat-called and abused in the street and finally the bastards killed Wally's gun-dog, Jess." Ben suddenly realized that he hadn't noticed that Jess wasn't there to meet him at the door, like he usually did, when Ben had arrived at Wally's house. That must have really got to Wally, Ben thought, he'd trained Jess from a pup and he loved his dog.

Ben was trying to comprehend what his brother was going through, when Wally re-emerged from the back room. His nose was red and swollen. He dabbed it with a blood stained piece of lint. Wally quickly realised that Ross had told Ben the story. Before Ben could say anything, Wally walked up close to his younger brother. Clasping his hand behind the back of Ben's head, he looked him in the eyes and quietly said,

" I don't want you to get involved in this, and I don't want to talk about this at all while you're at home, you understand?" Ben nodded in reluctant agreement. They both finished their pint and left for home.

The rest of Ben's leave seemed a little strange. No mention was made of the incident in the Ty Inn or of the union problems that Wally was going through in work. When it was finally time for Ben to drive back to camp, he tried to bring up the subject. Wally wouldn't get drawn. As he got into his battered Escort, Ben looked into the rapidly aging eyes of his brother. Wally smiled at him and told him everything would be OK and not to worry. Ben pulled slowly out of the cul-de-sac, where Wally lived. He tried to convince himself that Wally was all right and everything would sort itself out. Ben was confused and annoyed it had got to this level and he hadn't been able to help his big brother.

CHAPTER 3

Ben Brownley pulled up outside the barrack block back at his base at Hemingsby. His mind had been mulling over the amazing events of his leave. During the drive back, unusually for Ben, he'd been tuned to Radio 4. There had been a couple of reports and interviews on the evening news, which give the distinct impression that what Wally had been experiencing was definitely not a one off. Just over half way on the journey back to Hemingsby, Ben had stopped at a transport cafe for a coffee. He'd picked up a newspaper and there were several articles in the inside pages which gave some ominous warnings. Unions, militancy, flying pickets were all due for an unwelcome return. To add to that Ben had overheard a couple of lorry drivers complaining about their union's grip on their working hours. Ben thought to himself that he must have been going around with his eyes shut to miss the obvious signs.

Ben knew he had to get ready for his move overseas. He had to put his brother's problems aside, well at least until he'd sorted his new job out. Duty came first, Ben thought to himself with some amusement. That was the first time for a long time he had thought that. He was still concerned for his brother but after all it was not that far from Wales and after all, he could ring home regularly. Of course, the most important task at that moment in time was to find Dixie and see what had been arranged for his farewell 'beercall' in the rugby club.

Dixie had done the business as regards to Ben's farewell party and beercall. Dixie had mustered all of the club's players plus most of the Sooties that Ben knew from the other squadrons. Laid on was a copious quantity of beer, which was consumed with great vigor. Many songs of the more vulgar nature rung out, as is the norm at gatherings at the rugby club. To cap that a strip-a-gram turned up to entertain the lads by discarding, slowly and evocatively, her policewoman's uniform. Unfortunately just when she reached the point of removing the final, flimsy article of apparel, the lights went out! A power cut had deprived the baying audience of the climax of her performance. At the time Ben, like everyone, was unaware that the power cut was another indication of the problems that were trade union created. There would be many more problems to follow.

Ben couldn't really remember much of the evening, due to the vast quantity of foaming ale he had personally consumed. However in the morning the mother of all hangovers had let Ben know exactly what he had got up to the night before.

Ben had a day or two to recover from the festivities in the rugby club, before he had to report to Luton airport for the military trooper flight directly into RAF Feldbruch. Dixie came to see Ben off on the day he was due to be picked up by MT. He told Ben to sort out a decent room in the barrack block for him, when he got out to Feldbruch and set the beers up in the rugby club. Dixie waved off Ben with his usual two-fingered salute.

The minibus dropped Ben off at the airport. After the usual standard military waiting time of several uneventful hours had elapsed, Cpl Ben Brownley was blasted skywards towards his new posting in Germany.

At Royal Air Force Feldbruch in the North Rhine Westfallia district of Germany the trooper flight finally rolled to a halt. It was dwarfed by the large aircraft servicing pan that it was parked on. The aircraft rapidly disgorged its human payload, most of which were new arrivals to Germany. The usual customs formalities had to be observed and accommodation was allocated by a gormless looking, spotty-faced RAF policeman. Another minibus ride followed for Ben, this time a left hand drive version. It whisked Ben and his baggage to the barrack block, which would be his new home for the next three years. The barrack block, as were most of the buildings on the station, was tucked amongst hundreds of tall pine trees. The uniformed green- painted buildings melted easily into nature's own camouflage.

Ben partially unpacked his kit in the sparsely furnished room he had been allocated. He made a mental note to get some posters and pictures up on the wall to take away the plain and boring decor that the room offered. Within an hour he was making his way to the NAAFI bar for his first authentic German beer. On the way over to the NAAFI building complex he bumped into a guy he knew from training school. It turned out to be his next-door neighbour in the block. His name was Andy Lewington. He was a rigger, or to give him his correct trade, an airframe technician. Andy was posted into 701 Squadron as well. He had arrived the day or so before and he knew where most things where on the station. He also had his own wheels, so Ben latched on to him.

They both walked to the NAAFI bar for the obligatory quiet pint. The bar was very busy and the evening rushed past in a beery blur. Eventually the Orderly Corporal arrived to do his final rounds around midnight to throw out the last drinkers. Ben and Andy had clearly underestimated the strength of German beer. They were experiencing a little difficulty in standing upright and coordinating any sort of walking action. Ben did eventually manage to struggle back to his room and he collapsed onto his still unmade bed. When he woke up in the following morning, he found himself in the same position. His lips were almost stuck together and his breath stank: evident from the bloody awful taste that lingered in his mouth.

Ben had overslept and had missed breakfast. "Not a good start to his new job," he thought to himself, "Hungry and hung-over." Cpl Brownley went to Station Headquarters to start his arrival procedure. Tradition demands in the Air Force, as it has since Pontius was a pilot, that Corporal Brownley, as with all new arrivals, had to trudge for miles around the station to register his existence on the unit by collecting signatures on a blue coloured card. A complete waste of time, effort and shoe leather in today's age of the computer, Ben thought to himself. However it had consumed most of the morning and allowed Ben to clear his head and get some solids inside his stomach from the NAAFI canteen. The afternoon had been set aside for the numerous arrival briefings. Corporal Brownley was not looking forward to several hours of boring briefings with a potential death by 35mm slides and viewgraphs.

There were twenty or so new 701 Squadron personnel at the briefings. Ben was bored, almost to the point of dropping off to sleep at the endless procession of briefings, warnings and advice on how to conduct himself whilst in Germany. However Ben did perk up when the station commander came to give his welcoming address. The confident and commanding manner in which the Group Captain gave his own views on how he expected his new charges should conduct themselves on his station greatly impressed Ben. Corporal Brownley was not that interested to hear the role of the unit or how the future closure of the Germany bases was now a commitment. It wasn't until the Group Captain reassured everyone present, that they all could expect to complete their full three years tour that Ben took any notice. He clearly registered that particular important fact. However, when the subject of 701 Squadron came up in the proceedings, Ben did really take active interest.

The Group Captain explained, that following the Defence Review it was decided that new squadrons, like 701 Squadron, would be formed to fill the role within the new Rapid Reaction Force. It, unfortunately, required the disbandment of old squadrons, many of which had very long and distinguished histories. The new radical MOD policy did not go down well with the majority of the Brass in the Air Force. But the new Labour Party meant new government, new ideas and apparently a new Air Force. It would happen and that was that. The Group Captain confirmed that he acknowledged that it would require a considerable effort by all the station personnel to get the 701 Squadron operational. It would be hard work but it would be a very interesting and challenging time.

When Cpl Brownley left the briefing room he was a much wiser man. He finally knew why he'd been posted to Feldbruch and was definitely looking forward to his tour. He could put behind him the cock-ups and bollockings of the past. A new job. A new future. Maybe even promotion. Providing that Burton's threat to scupper that possibility did not come to fruition.

Corporal Brownley spent the next few weeks on the squadron dispersal. It consisted of numerous engineering and domestic buildings. The site was, however, dominated by twelve Harden Aircraft Shelters individually known as a HAS. Each could house one Tornado aircraft. They gave blast protection to the aircraft, aircrew and groundcrew. Aircraft could be refueled, rearmed and with engines running inside the HAS, they could taxy out ready for take off. They had been regarded in the early seventies as the ultimate in aircraft protection measures. However the Gulf war sadly proved their vulnerability.

Thirty other troops and the half a dozen aircrew soon arrived on the dispersal. 701 Squadron was growing rapidly towards its full peacetime strength of 140 personnel. For the first few weeks the engineers were headed by the squadron's newly appointed Warrant Officer, WO O'Reilly. He was soon christened O'Really O'Reilly by the groundcrew. This was due to the frequency, with which he used the phrase: " Oh really is that a fact?" in his conversation. He was a ruddy-faced Irishman with more than a touch of blarney about him. He had organized most of the troops into work parties. They were needed to sort out tools, ground equipment and the multitude of notice boards that adorn any engineering set-up.

For his sins Corporal Brownley had been given his first job. He had been allocated three young airmen to sort out the airman's tea bar and locker room. A cushy little number, Ben thought to himself, and plenty of mugs of coffee.

The preparation of the dispersal stretched past the first full month. A few more Senior NCOs had arrived and several more aircrew had pitched up on the squadron. The aircrew, as always, were a real pain in the arse. They had the squadron but it had no aircraft yet to zoom around in and punch holes in the sky with.

During this time, Ben had been keeping a wary eye on the situation back at home. The tension between the unions had been welling up and disruptive industrial action was commonplace. The power workers had continued selective power cuts; just like the night of his farewell beercall. The dustbin men seemed only to collect the rubbish when they felt like it. To add to these disruptions the rail unions compounded the problems of the general public by calling wildcat strikes whenever, and wherever they felt like it.

The media had widely reported that the Government where in negotiation with union leaders and a settlement was expected soon. No one believed that the government had the stomach for a fight. The left wing element of the party were slowly regaining their past status. The rank and file had grown in considerable numbers and began to dictate, through the more militant Labour MPs, governmental industrial policy. The Prime Minister's popularity as leader, after only a few years, was possibly on the wane. Ben could see a fresh winter of discontent looming.

Ben had rung home each week. Wally answered the phone most of the time, but Ben couldn't really tell how his brother was coping with the events back home. Wally still wouldn't discuss the matter at all. On one occasion Sarah answered the phone. She said Wally was out but Ben could sense a quiver in her voice. She also confided to Ben that his brother was deeply upset how things had turned out with his work. To make matters worse the newly elected head of the T&GWU for the Wrexham District turned out to be Keith Reece. Wally and Keith had been inseparable as best mates at school together, as they had grown up from toddlers to teenagers in the same street. Remarkably they were both so much physically alike that they were often mistaken for twins. But as so often happens as mates grow up, start courting and eventually get married, they drift apart. Wally hadn't seen much of Keith for many years, ever since their equally strong views on unions took them both on different paths. It now appeared that most of the impetus for the militancy and strike action in the Wrexham and, in particular, the local area of Brymbo, came from Keith Reece. This really saddened Wally.

To keep his mind off the problems at home, Ben had made many impressive appearances at the rugby training sessions each Tuesday evening. He knew several of the players from playing against them in the past. The young lad, who was the team's first choice for hooker, was a bit of a lard barrel. By the look of the way he handled the ball he'd been issued with Teflon coated fingers. Ben was very confident that he would swiftly replace him on the team. One of the props was fairly decent. However the other would not give Dixie very much opposition for the position. Training was hard work and very physical. Ben loved the sessions, which were always followed by the odd refreshing beer. The odd beer usually meant seven, nine or sometimes even eleven!

The Team Coach was chatting to Ben in the clubhouse one evening after training when Ben suddenly heard the dulcet tones of Dixie Dean emanating from behind him. Looking round, there he was, larger than life and twice as ugly. Dixie smiled and greeted his mate with his usual, "What d'ye know, what d'ye say, Benny boy?"

Ben was mildly but pleasantly shocked to see his mate.

"What are you doing here so early?" enquired Ben as he instinctively passed over a freshly opened bottle of Warsteiner beer that he'd pulled from a crate beneath the table. "I thought you weren't due out for another month," Ben added.

Dixie took a long slow swig of beer. Finally he put the bottle down and he wiped the froth of his top lip with the back of his hand. He stood admiring the empty bottle in his hand,

"Ah. Warstiener 'Wobbly', absolute nectar to my tonsils, " Dixie said with a passion. He looked at Ben, gestured for another beer and explained, "Well, you see Benny, due to the lefty union head-bangers, the whole of the UK seems to be held to ransom. Power cuts were coming so often we could hardly get anything done at work." Dixie took another long draught of beer and continued: " I spoke to the Flight Sergeant and asked if I could come over here early. You know me, Benny. Always keen to be hard at work, " he added with a cheeky grin.

Ben was extremely pleased to see his mate and drinking partner. Things just couldn't be better, he thought to himself.

"One thing that puzzles me" inquired Ben, "How did you manage to convince Burton to let you pull your posting forward?"

Dixie reached for yet another bottle of beer. It looked as if it was going to be a long, night. Dixie replied cheerily that it hadn't been a problem, as Burton had been posted away on promotion. Ben frowned at the thought of Burton as a Squadron Leader.

The next day, Ben took Dixie down to the dispersal after he had completed the mandatory foot-slogging arrival process. He was shown the layout of the squadron dispersal. Ben had even managed to wangle Dixie on to the same work party.

A few days later Ben's motley team of workers were walking out to the transport at lunchtime. Ben saw one of the junior pilots coming out of the aircrew accommodation. He beckoned Ben over. The young officer spoke in an unconvincing, commanding manner as he waved a piece of paper under Ben's nose.

"Cpl Brownley. I want you to take this over to the Paint Shop and ask if they can make and paint the new squadron sign."

Ben was just about to waffle some excuses to get himself out of running the young Pilot Officer's errands, when Dixie butted in. In his normally cheery, patronizing manner he said, " Of course, Sir, lets have a look at what the new sign is. After all, we're part of this squadron too, aint we, Sir?"

The paper showed the coloured drawing of the new squadron crest. It was studiously examined by the small posse of inquisitive groundcrew. The young officer explained that the new squadron commander had designed the crest himself. With an air of authority he said that it represented the new role of the squadron.

"How's that then, Sir?" Ben enquired. By now he had caught on to what Dixie was up to. The officer obviously was delighted in telling the airman all he knew about the new design. Ben thought the young officer must have been almost wetting himself to unload the burden of information that he thought he, alone, was privy too.

"Well you see," the young officer pontificated, "The globe with the lightning flash through it represents the role of the squadron - To be highly mobile and strike anywhere in the world. And as we'll be the leading squadron in the Rapid Reaction Force, it's very appropriate, don't you think?"
Dixie tried to suppress a chuckle, as he pointed to the Latin motto underneath the crest.

"And what does this mean, Sir"? he said, quizzing the young officer.

"Oh yes, I know that" said the now very excited, young pilot officer. "It's Latin." Dixie interrupted, the officer who was in full flow explanation mode.

" You don't say, aint it just amazing what they teach our intrepid aviators at Cranwell these days?"
The officer gave Dixie a glaring, black look and continued. " It says. "Nullum Ubi Probatur Melius," which, when literally translated, means, 'None better when tested.'

Ben Brownley turned away and shook his head almost in disbelief.

"What a load of bollocks," Ben whispered to Dixie. Ben and Dixie could see a golden opportunity to get one over the aircrew, which everyone knew was the sworn duty of all groundcrew. It did not offer itself very often, therefore the chance had to grasped with both hands. They took charge of the precious drawing and promised the officer they would personally ensure that the new squadron sign would be manufactured. And, of course, it would be suitably erected outside the squadron HQ.

As the team travelled over to the paint shop, Ben was searching for some way to score points over the aircrew. He tentatively suggested that maybe they should alter the design so as to drop the young officer in the mire. However Dixie was hatching a cunning plan. Ben could always tell by the expression on his mate's face. It was a sort of cross between confusion and constipation. Dixie suddenly exclaimed that he had the answer. All the team waited, hovering in anticipation, for him to divulge the devious scam that he'd just hatched. Dixie said nothing. He jumped out of the vehicle and scampered off into the paint shop. He did not reappear for twenty minutes or so. Each and every person in the vehicle was busting to know what he had done. Dixie sat smugly on the seat and declared that all would be revealed in time. Everyone was going to just have to wait and see, he added defiantly. Dixie would not budge on that. Not even to his best mate, Ben. Dixie finally admitted in his usual cheeky and mischievous voice, "It's a surprise."

The work to get the squadron ready to accept its aircraft continued at a relentless pace. Adding to the ever-swelling nominal role of 701 Squadron was the new Jengo. Flight Lieutenant Brian Simpson was a young, ebullient character who made an instant and favourable impact on the groundcrew. His pleasant, friendly manner succeeded in giving a necessary impetus to the engineers. The squadron and its dispersal were almost ready to accept the new inventory of GR5 aircraft. The Jengo soon attracted his inevitable nickname. He was affectionately christened after a cartoon character. So Flight Lieutenant 'Bart' Simpson was duly enrolled on the squadron by the groundcrew. Ben was struck by the quantum difference between Bart Simpson and Julian Burton, his last Jengo. Of course Ben knew exactly, which he would rather work for.

A couple of days before the new Wing Commander was due to fly in with the first of the squadron's aircraft, Corporal Brownley was detailed as the Squadron Duty Driver. Ben was waiting one lunch time to take the troops over to the domestic area of the station. They needed to go to airman's mess for their mid- day meal. Suddenly, the squadron dispersal PA system blared out around the empty HAS's. It summoned Cpl Brownley to the Warrant Officer.

When Brownley entered the office, Warrant Officer O'Reilly spoke in his soft Irish brogue,

"And where are you off to young Brownley"? enquired Warrant Officer O'Reilly.

"I'm off to the mess with the troops. Then I'm going to the NAAFI shop, Sir. " Brownley replied. Somewhat predictably, the Warrant Officer responded with:

"Oh really is that a fact? Well, I want you to go and collect the new Sengo from his married quarters and bring him back here before you shoot off to the NAAFI. Here's the address, and look lively about it."

Brownley drove the Landrover off the squadron dispersal. He dropped the boys off at the Airman's Mess and then drove around to the address he had been given. The Landrover pulled outside the almost palatial senior officer's house. The usual signs of a recent house move could be seen. Empty packing cases lay around the garden and inside the open garage.

Cpl Brownley walked up the short path and knocked sharply on the front door. He was a little inquisitive and actually looking forward to meeting his new Sengo. A few moments later the door was opened and to Brownley's surprise, by an extremely pretty teenage girl. She had long blonde hair, big inviting brown eyes and a figure that certainly would attract more than a passing glance from any hot-blooded male.

Ben was quite taken by the young girl and chatted away on the doorstep to her for several minutes. He'd almost forgotten what he had come for. He soon found out that the girl's name was Samantha. Ben was quite shocked to learn that Samantha was only fourteen and still at school. His interest and his ardour was instantly cooled. He turned off his charm, as he thought to himself, "Pretty she might be but jail bait she definitely was."

Samantha must have sensed what Ben was thinking and she blushed a little. She shouted inside to her father that his driver had arrived to collect him. Cpl Brownley had returned back to the driver's seat by the time his passenger emerged through the front door. The Squadron Leader kissed young Samantha on the cheek and turned towards the Landrover.

Cpl Brownley's heart fell into his boots. His head dropped onto his arms, which were draped over the steering wheel. 701 Squadron's new Sengo was none other than, Squadron Leader Julian Burton.

CHAPTER 4

During the drive back to 701 Squadron's dispersal, Brownley clutched for words, with which to strike up a conversation with his passenger. But such suitable words evaded him. Ben did eventually find out, however, that Squadron Leader Burton was actually posted in at short notice. He had replaced the original Sengo, who had been nominated for the post. Unfortunately he had been injured in a car accident and would not be fit quickly enough to get the squadron operational.

Obviously Cpl Brownley was very keen to know how he stood in regards to his second tour under Burton's command. He tried desperately to conjure up the right approach to find the answer. Squadron Leader Burton didn't give away any clues of how he would be treating his sometimes, wayward subordinate. So Ben wasn't that optimistic about his future and he could just imagine what Dixie would make of the situation.

Ben told Dixie later on that afternoon about the arrival of their least favourite officer. His response was predictable. It was one word, comprising two short syllables - "Bollocks!" Several glasses of Warstiener 'Wobbly' beer would be the ideal remedy for such a situation, Dixie declared. Both agreed to drown their sorrows, but only after rugby training.

Training that evening produced an aggressive response from the two corporals. They hit the tackle bags with renewed venom. Both imagined a picture of Burton's face on the large canvas bag, which substituted for a rugby player. The coach looked on in disbelief. Never before had he seen his two star front-row forwards emit so much enthusiasm for tackling drills. They hit the club house bar with a similar vengeance that evening.

The following week Squadron Leader Julian Burton took over total command of all the engineering activities of the squadron. Up until that time the squadron had functioned extremely well with either the Jengo or Warrant Officer in charge. However the Sengo's domineering, autocratic management style changed the way of things. Morale amongst the groundcrew took a dip. The troops resented the change, which they saw as unnecessary. They now did what they did because they had to not because they wanted to. Jengo Simpson frequently stood up for the groundcrew. However it was more often than not completely in vain. He had already received quite a few closed-door discussions from the Sengo. Everyone knew that it was because Burton wanted him to be more forceful and demanding of the troops. But that wasn't Bart Simpson's style. He managed to get damn good value and hard graft out the troops by helping them and encouraging them. Burton seemed to resent his Jengo's popularity.

Within the next few days the first of the new GR5 aircraft arrived. The Wing Commander flew the lead aircraft into RAF Feldbruch. After all the newly arrived aircraft had been refueled and serviced, 701 Squadron had its first squadron beercall. Every member of the squadron had assembled in one of the HASs. Several barrels of beer had been provided, courtesy of the aircrew, and that was almost a first in Brownley's experience. It was meant as a sweetener for the task ahead. With shift-work starting the following week it was the only opportunity they would have for a great big piss-up for quite some time.

The party was a very boisterous affair. If not a little out of hand at times. As the beer was rapidly consumed, Ben and Dixie led the singing. They were also the main instigators of many of the stupid games that can happen during beer calls. Unfortunately things did get well out of hand. Both the young corporals downed for a dare, a yard of beer mixed with a whole bottle of tobasco sauce. It prompted a rapid and colourful response first by Dixie, who was very swiftly followed by Ben. They disgorged the contents of their stomach in an almost synchronized five-finger spread. Sadly their unintentional recipients were the Wing Commander and the Sengo who were standing nearby. The party stopped abruptly and everyone drifted off home.

The following day both Cpls Brownley and Dean were in the Sengo's office for the first of many bollockings. It was deja vu for Ben and Dixie. They both expected formal disciplinary action to be taken. Thankfully the Wing Commander wanted to keep the incident in-house. He saw no point in broadcasting a minor, distasteful occurrence to the whole station. Squadron Leader Burton had made his views crystal clear to his two corporals. He just would not tolerate their same unexceptable level of behavior that he'd previously witnessed at Hemingsby. Following the torrent of criticism heaped on Ben and Dixie by the Sengo, they were awarded the task of cleaning up the crewroom and the toilets. It was to be supervised by W.O. O'Reilly. He was not over-impressed by the task he was given by the Sengo and even less impressed by the performance of two of his corporals.

It was only just over two months before an important exercise that would measure the tactical ability of the squadron. Squadron Leader Burton was driving the engineers hard to provide the maximum number of aircraft, serviced in the minimum time. The only respite for the engineers was when the Jengo ran the shift. He was pragmatic about the task. He managed to achieve the same result that Burton did but without the hassle or aggravation, which was seen as the Sengo's trademark.

The aircrew were flying hard. Their confidence and achievement to become fully operational as a squadron was well on target. It often resulted in long hours to prepare the aircraft for the next day's flying. This was generally understood as an essential part of the job by all of the groundcrew. Even though the squadron was still in its infancy, a squadron spirit had emerged... despite Burton's efforts to suppress it.

The following week it was Dixie's turn to be tasked as the Squadron Duty Driver. He returned to the dispersal one afternoon with the newly painted squadron sign fresh from the Paint Shop. The aircrew gathered around Dixie in curious anticipation. He expertly screwed the spanking-new squadron crest to the wall of the Squadron HQ building. When he had finished, he left the aircrew posing together for photographs for the squadron's scrapbook.

Dixie then produced another freshly painted sign from the back of the Landrover. This one he screwed to the wall of the ground crew accommodation. A gaggle of engineers gathered around to see what Dixie had conjured up. He'd done a deal with the painters, which as usual, had involved the exchange of a crate of beer. The painters and finishers had manufactured a large sign, which had the 701 Squadron groundcrew crest emblazoned on it. Its unveiling was met with unanimous approval and hoots of delight from all of the gathered masses. Dixie had parodied the resplendent effort of the Wing Commander with one of his own. The globe and lightning strike had been substituted with a half lemon impaled by a corkscrew. The fancy motto, in English this time, had also been transposed from: 'None Better When Tested' to 'All Bitter and Twisted.'

All the engineers saw the funny side of the prank. It demonstrated the universal warped sense of humour, which most servicemen enjoyed. Such a sense of humour could keep the troops going, when things weren't going too well. The W.O. and Jengo both tolerated the presence of the newly erected groundcrew crest. They recognized that it helped to maintain morale amongst the groundcrew. After the hectic times of the past weeks: morale had taken a severe hammering. However the Sengo had a complete 'sense of humour failure' over the sign. He ordered its immediate removal. He particularly did not like the newly adopted groundcrew motto. Although it had been invented by Cpl Dean well before his arrival, its aptness in the light of Burton's effect on the groundcrew was all too close to the truth.

The Wing Commander decided the ground crew crest could stay. This news was received with much delight by all the troops. Rumour control had it, that O'Really O'Reilly had a hand in it. A timely word from a Warrant Officer to a

Wing Commander would usually sway a decision in favour of the Warrant's suggestion. Shortly afterwards cloth badges depicting the groundcrew crest and motto were obtained to adorn the green overalls that the groundcrew wore. For some strange reason Sqn Ldr Burton wouldn't buy one!

One evening, Ben Brownley came into work to start night shift. He picked up his mail from the crewroom. There was a letter from home and it was in Sarah's handwriting. It was unusual, as normally Sarah never wrote to Ben. The letter revealed the latest problems that Wally had endured at work. The union shop steward had been having another go at Wally for his refusal to comply with the union's directives. Sarah was convinced that her husband was heading for a nervous breakdown. But Wally wouldn't see a doctor nor would he give up his job. Sue also admitted that Wally had been beaten up at work again. His car had been dowsed in battery acid and a poison pen letter had been pushed through his front door. Sarah wrote in her letter that Wally was utterly convinced that Keith Reece was calling the shots and dispatching his henchmen to do his bidding against anyone, who wouldn't tow the union party line.

Ben was worried about his brother... he just had to go home to see him. The Christmas stand-down was only a fortnight away and Ben had hoped to get away before then for some leave. However, bewildering news from Squadron Leader Burton had put a stop to all leave before Christmas. The squadron was down on the target for the monthly flying hours. And it was obvious that more flying sorties had to be completed before the Christmas holiday. Flight Lieutenant

Simpson argued in Brownley's favour but the Sengo wouldn't budge.

The day before the 701 Squadron finally stood down for Christmas the radio in the crewroom announced an item of news, which completely dismayed Ben. The Seaman's Union and Dockers were to start an immediate strike and all UK ports would close to all shipping and ferries. This would also be supported by Union of the Channel Tunnel rail-link workers. Ben was incensed. In his eyes Wally's condition was as a result of the union's bullyboy tactics. Their totally selfish attitude showed they were hell-bent on spoiling everyone's Christmas as well. Ben's only option to get home would be by air. With such short notice not one seat was available before Christmas and to make things worse the Sengo issued a squadron policy decision to ensure everyone would be available for work at the start of the new year. It stated that, unless squadron personnel had a guaranteed return air ticket, leave would not be granted to go back to the UK.

Trade union leaders appeared on t.v. and their grievances were reported on numerous radio interviews. The tabloid press also had mass coverage of the dispute almost every day. The union leaders openly boasted of their challenge against management. They made it clear that they intended to continue industrial action and repeat it until they got what they wanted. There were loud calls from opposition politicians to recall Parliament during the Christmas recess, but this was swiftly dismissed by a Government spokesman, as unnecessary.

Ben rang home that evening. He spoke to Wally, who finally did start to open up and talk about the union troubles that had plagued him for so long. It would have been hard to avoid now, as it dominated all the news and papers. To Ben his brother sounded OK. But Wally had developed an occasional stutter. It was only noticeable, when he talked about the unions or the trouble they were maliciously inflicting on the whole country. Ben was still worried about his brother but he resigned himself that Christmas would have to be spent at Feldbruch. Not the ideal situation and it could have been worse but as far as Ben was concerned at that time, not much worse.

Ben and Dixie made the best of the predicament in which they found themselves. Most of the holiday was spent in the rugby clubhouse. Many people were in the same, exiled position so the clubhouse was packed most of the time. Christmas diner was a barbecue consumed in the freezing cold outside the clubhouse. The clubhouse's profits rocketed, as the bar never seemed to shut. For once the RAF Police turned a blind eye to the flexible opening hours that would have normally been stamped on. Even the Station Commander popped in for a beer on Boxing Day. He came along to watch the quickly- arranged charity rugby match. It saw the Station team play against a team of ladies. It soon became very apparent that their tackling and mauling could teach the men's team a lesson or two. However the men's team defiantly had the edge when it came to the after-match singing.

The highlight of the Christmas break culminated in the New Year's Eve fancy dress party. After all it was to be the start of the new millennium. As Germany was one hour ahead of the United Kingdom, all Brits got to celebrate the arrival of the year 2000 at midnight in both countries. The clubhouse was rocking and throbbing from lunch time onwards. Entry into the party was free but only if fancy dress was worn. A crate of beer was the mandatory entrance fee for any one who wasn't wearing some form of fancy dress.

Ben turned up dressed as Uncle Fester a ghoulish character from the Adams Family. He was dressed in a long, black coat, combat boots with a white swimming cap on his head. He only needed to add dark rings around his eyes and he was a spitting image of the real thing. Dixie, as always, went right over the top and came as Sammy the Sperm. He wore a white balaclava helmet with white tee-shirt and long johns. A long white tail dangled from his backside, which completed the outfit. Not many people recognized immediately what he was supposed to be. However he took great delight, especially with the females, to explain who he was.

As the party consumed the remains of the century, Ben and Dixie circulated, chatted to the women and drank with their mates. Ben could not completely ignore the problems of his brother even on that night. He'd promised himself to ring home after midnight. Far too many Warstiener beers erased that promise as the evening passed.

Just before midnight, German time, Ben saw someone in the bar, whom he recognized. In the corner three or four young girls were standing, smoking and drinking. One of them was the girl he had seen outside Burton's house. It was Samantha, the Sengo's daughter. Ben knew she was under age to be in the clubhouse and he also knew that under age drinking was one sure way to get the place closed. To make it worse her nurse's fancy dress costume left very little to the imagination.

Ben went over to her. She met him with a smile and she blushed a little. He knew that the rugby clubhouse was not a place for an underage teenage girl when it was full of lustful, drunken airmen and suggested that she should go home with her mates. Samantha Burton pouted her well-glossed lips at him and laughed. As she turned away she said to Ben,

" You sound like my father."

Ben was thunderstruck. It was a sobering thought, as he contemplated the image of himself as Julian Burton. At that moment his thoughts were rudely interrupted by Dixie who thrust a beer under his nose.

" Come on Benny Boy. Time for the fireworks," he said in a drunken drawl. Everyone soon gathered outside to see the fireworks display that Dixie had arranged. Standing on the grass outside there was an empty forty-five gallon oil drum with the top taken off. Dixie explained to his awaiting audience that, in the interest of safety and to prevent damage to the hallowed turf of the rugby pitch, the drum would serve as the bonfire. He then dropped something inside it. Ben knew immediately that it was a thunderflash, as it sizzled and spluttered inside the echoing chamber of the drum. Most people were too drunk to realize as they eagerly awaited the mini bonfire to ignite. A few seconds later a vivid flash an ear-shattering explosion punctured the dark night air. It startled everyone and made the women scream with delight. Dixie had filled the drum with gunge made from water, flour and food colouring. The explosion had initiated a Krakatoan-type eruption. The bright green slime was ejected skywards into the darkness. It then rained down upon the awaiting audience. Dixie's cackling laughter was heard from behind the crowd. Everyone turned and ran towards the clubhouse to seek revenge on the prankster. But by now Dixie had climbed up onto the roof of the clubhouse and was armed with a fire extinguisher. He liberally sprayed the white foam onto the crowd below and called out.

"Happy New Year. " A huge cheer ran out and revenge against Dixie was instantly forgotten. The Year 2000 had arrived. Dixie had been forgiven as hugs, kisses and handshakes were exchanged. In the distance real fireworks displays could be heard and occasionally seen in the skies as the millennium was celebrated in the many villages that surrounded the airbase.

One hour later midnight in UK was celebrated in a similar fashion but without the pyrotechnics provided by Dixie. The party continued into the first early hours of the New Millennium. Many people eventually drifted back to their rooms and houses. But many stayed and found any suitable spot to gab a few hours combat kip.

As daylight speared through the gap in the curtains, Ben woke up on the clubhouse floor along with several other party-goers. His head was remarkably clear, at first and it started to reverberate like the oil drum when the thunderflash went off the previous evening.

Ben went back to his room to sleep-off the rest of the Christmas holiday. He was due back to work in two days. He hoped that his hang-over would clear in time.

CHAPTER 5

The Christmas holiday was soon over and Ben Brownley had to return to work. He had managed to ring home on New Years Day and had spoken to his brother. Wally said that he'd had a pleasant Christmas but Ben was not all that convinced. There still seemed to be a slight waver in Wally's voice and his stammer was more pronounced, when he did speak of the union troubles at home.

Ben had to concentrate on his work. He knew until the port strikes were lifted he could not contemplate a visit home. Flying home still might be a possibility but Ben would have to pick his time carefully. Work was due to start on Tuesday the 4th of January. Ben was on B shift and they were on nights starting that week. So he had a chance to go for a run with Dixie. They needed to try and work off the festive over-indulgence, of which they had both been extremely guilty.

The first shift back on the squadron was very busy. It set the scene for the rest of January and the aircrew was very keen to fly, after the holiday layoff. The aircraft misbehaved, as they always do, after being on the ground instead of flying. They went unserviceable after every flight and long hours of rectification and repairs were needed to make them available for the next day's flying. The Sengo was in his element. He charged around shouting at the SNCOs and demanding more serviceable aircraft. Everyone was getting a little bit pissed off with his constant drive to meet the flying programme.

Leading Aircraftsman Kelvin Gunter was one of the squadron linies and he was sat in the crewroom drinking coffee that afternoon. He was known as Egor by everyone, including the Wing Commander, on account of his striking resemblance to the horror film actor Peter Lorre. Egor had been, in the finest traditions of groundcrew, 'earwigging' at the Sengo's office door, after the Warrant Officer had been summoned by Squadron Leader Burton. 'Evesdroper Egor' had overheard W.O. O'Reilly arguing with the Sengo over the way the groundcrew were been driven. Squadron Leader Burton threatened to throw O'Really O' Reilly off the squadron, unless he improved the performance of all of the groundcrew. Egor told everyone in the crewroom what he had heard. But many of the SNCOs didn't believe that the Sengo would threaten the Warrant. Ben and Dixie knew from past experience that Burton was capable of anything.

January passed with the squadron working hard and easily achieving the monthly flying hours target. The aircrew was happy and this prompted the Wing Commander to pop into the airmen's crewroom one morning. He personally thanked everyone present for the tremendous effort by everyone to get the squadron ready for the important evaluation exercise, which was due in a few weeks.

The Sengo slid into the crewroom and sat down in the corner to listen to what the Winco had to say. Sqn Ldr Burton stood up to address the groundcrew after the Wing Commander had left the crewroom. He announced the change of shift pattern, which would start the following week. It came as a shock to everyone included, by the looks on their faces, the Jengo and Warrant Officer. The new schedule would mean 12-hour shifts for A and B shift. They would run from six to six each day and night. This provided the maximum availability of engineering personnel to provide the aircraft that the Sengo demanded but it completely screwed up their social lives. The proposed shifts were often used but only on detachment or for short periods of time. Burton's plan was to run them right up to the major exercise in September. It would give him the aircraft he craved but at the expense of the groundcrew. The decision went down like a lead balloon.

Ben and Dixie in particular were less than pleased with the new shifts because it gave them very limited chances to play rugby for the station on Wednesdays. Up to that time they had managed to get regular games. With help from Jengo Simpson, both had played, when scheduled for night shift and on most day shifts, when the flying programme permitted. They were even more aggrieved, when they found out that trials for the RAF Senior side were imminent and the selection committee was looking for potential players. The Coach mentioned that both Ben and Dixie were in with a chance of selection for the trial, if they could produce the goods during the next couple of station games. It looked like Burton's new shift ideas would put paid to that.

The following week, A and B shift ground crew were ushered into one of the HASs at shift change-over time for a briefing. It was only a week before the important evaluation exercise. This would indicate to the Station Commander and to the NATO top brass whether the squadron was progressing at sufficient pace to become fully operational following the Tactical Evaluation or Taceval as it was known to everyone.

That evaluation exercise was due to be held in September. Most of the briefing was boring and talked of flying operations and weapon loads. However what did register with the groundcrew was the fact that everyone, except the aircrew of course, would be sleeping on the squadron dispersal and no one would be permitted to leave the site until after the exercise. A ripple of disapproval spread around the audience. The Jengo had yet again been taken by surprise by the Sengo's announcement. The dispersal didn't really have the facilities to house everyone. Also the noise of aircraft operating would mean there would be little or no sleep for the off-duty shift. Rumour had it that it was the Sengo's own brainchild and he was determined to see it realized.

The weekend before the exercise saw frantic activity on 701 Squadron's dispersal. Most of the trades were working both Saturday and Sunday to prepare the aircraft in readiness for the start of the exercise or Startex at 0600 hours on Monday. Working Saturday meant that Ben and Dixie would miss the first of the season's Home International rugby matches. It was also to be the first season that Italy where to be included into the famous annual event. Therefore The Five Nations competition had now become Six. The opening game was between England and Wales. It was eagerly looked forward to by both Ben and Dixie, who would be supporting their respective countries. The game was scheduled to be screened on Sky TV in the rugby clubhouse. Ben and Dixie would unfortunately be sweating pints in work, instead of sinking them that afternoon in the clubhouse.

Squadron Leader Burton came up with another gem of inspiration. He decided that all aircraft would be fully armed up and loaded with the designated bomb load on the day before the exercise. This would enable a rapid start to the flying and the squadron would score brownie points, as they would be ready to use the first slots on the bombing ranges. For the imminent exercise the bomb load would only comprise 14-kilogram practice bombs. During Taceval however, live 1000-pound high explosive bombs would be dropped on the ranges on the east coast of the UK. Regardless of the type of bomb to be loaded, Sengo Burton decided that the same procedures would be adopted as standard practice in preparation for Taceval.

When the aircraft were armed and loaded, the dispersal would have to be manned throughout the night. Of course, the RAF Police would do their usual security checks but the Sengo wanted the site guarded, open and ready for an early start. Warrant Officer O'Reilly asked for volunteers to stay over night and guard the site. He had no takers. Ben finally volunteered, before he was volunteered for the job by the Sengo. Dixie offered his services too as a gesture of solidarity. Secretly they both hoped that maybe it might help to redeem themselves in the eyes of Squadron Leader Burton.

Ben also realized an advantage of staying over the night before the exercise. It allowed Dixie and him to have first choice for a bed-space. They both selected a space in the hardened equipment shelter, which was to be the improvised dormitory for all future exercises. The spaces chosen for their camp beds and sleeping bags were well away from the door and near the heater.

Warrant Officer O'Reilly briefed his two corporals that evening. They had to do regular security checks on all armed aircraft and also to deliver the liquid oxygen containers, when they were ready, to each of the HAS's.

Finally he reminded them to ensure the HAS's were unlocked in time for shift start at 0600 hours. As O'Reilly was about to leave, he also tasked his two corporals to ensure the tractor was refueled in readiness for the exercise. He reminded them that the Ground Refueling Flight would only remain open until 2200 hours. It would not be open during the exercise, except for emergencies.

Darkness fell over 701 Squadron's dispersal early on that Sunday evening. Corporals Brownley and Dean had just finished another of their security rounds, when they bumped into the RAF Police Dog Handler as he started his night shift. Dixie immediately could see a way of delegating the onerous job of site security. What better guard could they have then a snarling, 90 lb. police dog. It would prove an irresistible deterrent to any would-be intruder. Dixie worked his charms on the policeman and between them they agreed to keep indoors, while the dog was 'off lead ' on the dispersal. The handler would then lock up the dog so Ben and Dixie could then deliver the liquid oxygen pots after they had been recharged, which would be about midnight.

Ben and Dixie were contented with the fact that with a Police Dog patrol on the squadron site, the dispersal would be safe from any uninvited guests. After all, the RAF Police were competent enough to do the security checks every other weekend. So why shouldn't it suffice that evening? Dixie produced a couple of tins of beer. They both knew that O'Reilly would have had a duck fit, if he found out that they'd had beer when on duty. Ben set up his TV and video in the crewroom. They settled down to watch the tape of the rugby match, which had been played at Twickenham the previous day.

The two corporals lazed away the evening and were pleasantly pleased with the way the night had evolved. At midnight a phone call was taken by Dixie. It was from the Oxygen Bay and it was to remind him that the oxygen pots were ready for collection.

Dixie left Ben in the crewroom, while he went off to collect the oxygen pots with the tractor and trailer. A few minutes later Dixie returned. He poked his head through the crewroom doorway and spoke to Ben, who was seated, feet up, in front of the t.v.

"Benny Boy, me old mate," asked Dixie. " What were we supposed to do with the tractor tonight?"
After a short pregnant silence Ben exclaimed,

"Oh bollocks, the soddin' tractor needs refueling."

"Spot on, Benny Boy. There's nothing but Massey Ferguson on that fuel gauge," replied Dixie, as he gestured out of the door with his raised thumb. Dixie then added,

"And I reckon that Burton will definitely blow a head gasket, if the tractor is out of action for Startex tomorrow."

Ben slumped back in the chair. He racked his brains of how they were going to get fuel for the tractor. He tried ringing the refueling flight office but there was no answer. Ben and Dixie were, for once, at a complete loss at what to do. They sat down to a cup of coffee, as they tried to conjure up the look on Burton's face, when he discovers that the tractor was nearly out of fuel. He would have to go cap in hand to the OC Supply Squadron to ask for refueling flight to be opened specially for 701 Squadron. The Sengo and OC Supply had been known to have a little disagreement in the past and since then never did quite see eye to eye.

As dawn approached Dixie was staring out of the crewroom window looking for divine intervention. He suddenly turned to Ben and with an ecstatic outburst he declared:

" I've got it, Benny Boy!"

"What are you on about?" asked Ben.

"Its easy, we'll syphon some diesel out of each of the Houchin electrical generator sets and top up the tractor's fuel tank." Dixie explained. With a beaming smile on his face he added, "Each of the generator's fuel tanks held over fifty litres of diesel. Syphoning off about ten litres from each set would not be noticed and the tractor could run for hours on that." He added urgently,

" Come on Benny Boy, Lets do it."

Both the corporals had suddenly been overcome with an urgent inject of enthusiasm. They ran around each HAS armed with a plastic pipe and Jerrycan. At the third HAS they set up the pipe and can to suck out the first draught of diesel from the generator's fuel tank. Being so engrossed in the task in hand, they did not realize that the Sengo had walked up into the HAS. Ben saw him first, just as Dixie was spitting out the diesel that had inadvertently entered his mouth, as he sucked to draw fuel down the tube. Ben nudged his oppose and whispered,

" Knock it off, Dixie. It looks like were in the shit again."

Dixie looked up in disbelief; his attention diverted towards their unexpected guest. With his head raised it meant he was unaware that the syphon tube was, at that time, functioning correctly. But instead of filling up the Jerrycan, it was slowly generating an ever-expanding inflammable puddle around his feet.

Squadron Leader Burton spoke to break the silence of the trio.

" I suppose I should have expected something like this would happen, when you two were left alone." Burton pointed to the puddle of fuel and added, now more tersely, " Now would you mind explaining to me what on earth you are up to?"

As Dixie mopped up the mess he had made, Cpl Brownley explained. They had to come clean and admitted that they had missed the refueling time for the tractor. So they knew that the only way to ensure the tractor would be available for the exercise was to take a little from each of the power sets.

Burton did admit that his two incorrigible corporals had, for once, shown some initiative. However he reminded them that their actions could have put the squadron's performance in jeopardy during the exercise. He walked away telling them both to finish what they had started and that he would deal with them after the exercise. Ben and Dixie were left to puzzle out if they had actually incurred the Sengo's wrath again or for once, impressed him.

Within the hour the rest of the groundcrew had arrived on the dispersal and were dressing in combats in preparation for the exercise. The day shift were preparing the aircraft while the night shift went into the shelter to get their heads down until shift change at 1800 hours. Cpl Brownley went to hand in the keys of the freshly refueled tractor to the Flight Sergeant, but he was intercepted by Warrant Officer O'Reilly. Resplendent in his well- pressed combats and highly polished boots, Warrant Officer O'Reilly approached Cpl Brownley and whispered in his ear:

"Well, young Brownley, did you look after my aircraft and remember to refuel the tractor?"

Ben replied with a slight hesitation,

"Yesser, of course, Sir."

His voice raised a few decibels as he backed away from Brownley's right ear, Warrant Officer O'Reilly retorted in time honoured fashion,

"Oh really, is that a fact?" After a suitable silence had elapsed to give his statement full effect he added, "Since when have generators been fuel suppliers for tractors?" It was obvious Sengo had relayed his early morning discovery to O'Reilly. The Warrant Officer told Brownley that yet again he and Cpl Dean had both let the squadron down. He confessed that he was really getting pissed off with the Sengo always complaining about the groundcrew. He added that Brownley and Dean had gone too far this time and should expect to receive a suitable punishment following the exercise.

The exercise in fact went extremely well and the aircrew had excelled themselves on the ranges and met all the bombing range slots they had been allocated. The aircraft stayed reasonably serviceable throughout the intense flying period. Unfortunately the aircraft that Ben and Dixie were responsible for was slow to be made ready for flight during an operational turn-round and re-arm. The Sengo stormed into the HAS to find out the reason for the delay. He chewed the weapon-loading team off a strip but his more scathing comments were aimed straight at Corporals Brownley and Dean.

The exercise had lasted just over 72 hours, and at 'Endex' the groundcrew were completely and utterly knackered to a man. It had been the first major trial of capability and endurance for the squadron. The Wing Commander addressed everyone during the exercise 'wash-up' de-briefing held in one of the HASs. He was very pleased how things had gone. However his genuine appreciation had been lost on the vast majority of the groundcrew as they were too tired to absorb his laudatory comments. After the briefing and whilst the post-exercise clean-up was under way, all the troops were moaning about the hectic and sometimes dangerous pace they had been driven at. There was universal agreement that the Sengo had pushed the groundcrew far too hard. Everybody was convinced that the two accidents, which had put one man in hospital and another in plaster, was believed by everyone to be down to the Sengo's over zealous requirements. The Jengo had tried to stop the exercise, because of the safety risk but Burton had over-ruled him.

If what had just been witnessed during the exercise by Cpl Brownley and all the other groundcrew, was just the start, what could the squadron expect during the Taceval exercise in September?

Both the NAAFI and the rugby clubhouse bars were very subdued places that evening. Beer was consumed at a controlled, sensible pace as the 701 Squadron groundcrew contemplated the extraordinary events that had occurred during the past three days. In the eyes of the troops the villain of the piece was definitely the Sengo.

Brownley had never really hated anyone. Sure he despised the union thugs who tormented his brother, but hate was a very emotive word. The Sengo, his actions and his low esteem towards the efforts of the groundcrew were now in the advanced stages of attracting that exact emotion from Brownley. Ben also had to consider that, maybe, Burton's feeling towards him were mutual.

CHAPTER 6

A week had passed since the exercise had finished. Finally the troops of 701 Squadron were beginning to recover their stamina. After the intense activities building up to that recent exercise, the Wing Commander had directed that a more relaxed regime would prevail, at least for a few weeks, before the start of the next intensive work up period towards Taceval. The shift hours reverted back to normal and even the Sengo had backed off a little. Unusually he permitted the occasional aircraft to lie unserviceable for a day or so instead of being fixed before the shift ended.

On the Friday both Ben and Dixie were summoned to the Sengo's office. They knew it was judgment time for their pre-exercise cock-up. Both corporals were brought to attention and under the ever-watchful eye of Warrant Officer O'Reilly, they awaited their just deserts. They were marched into Squadron Leader Burton's office and were halted in front of a large mahogany desk. He immediately switched into bollocking mode. It was almost like a loop tape as it sounded and felt like their last and all their other previous tirades that they had been subjected to. Burton concluded with his final summary judgment. Both would pick up extra duties, as selected by him and at a time that would probably be the most inconvenient for Ben and Dixie. Sengo Burton smirked slightly, when he announced that they would be told, in due course, what the duties entailed. When Burton had finished his deliberation, W.O. O'Reilly marched the two corporals out of the office.

Outside the office Dixie smiling at Ben commented that it could have been worse, as he thought they had got off lightly in the circumstances.

" Maybe," he added, "Burton had actually been impressed by our initiative after all."

Ben was not so optimistic about the punishment that they would soon be receiving. He announced that the extra duties were bound to be over Easter, the May Bank holidays or at some time that would stop him flying home to his brother. Dixie put his arm around Ben's shoulders and told him not to so bloody negative. They went back to the barrack block to get changed and to go out for a beer at the clubhouse.

When they got to the rugby club, several of the players were crowded around the notice board. Dixie couldn't see what they were all looking at. He ducked down and burrowed into the scrummage of bodies that lay before him. Seconds later, he emerged up in front of the notice board. Pinned to the middle of the board was a poster. It announced the details of the rugby club Easter tour. A list was attached for the names of those who wished to go. Dixie shouted out to Ben, who was standing at the back of the crowd,

"Benny Boy we're off on tour to Welsh Wales to teach your brother Taffies how to play God's favorite sport. I've added our names to the list, so get the beers in."

Dixie was ecstatic about the up and coming rugby tour. As they sat and sipped a beer together, he could see Ben was not that enthusiastic.

"What's the problem Benny?" asked Dixie.

Ben was certain that Burton would put the stoppers on the tour by putting them on extra duties and he told Dixie so. Dixie knew he had to cheer up his mate and snap him out of the bout of self-pity from which he was suffering.

"Now just wait a minute Benny Boy" Dixie implored. "You and me and the rest of the team will be going on tour, so Burton can go stuff himself as far as I'm concerned". Dixie then emptied the contents of his full pint glass in one swallow and gulp. He smiled at Ben and announced that it was his round again. Ben cracked a week smile and realized it was no point arguing with his mate. So he went to the bar for more beer.

The next two weeks saw a larger than usual and a very enthusiastic attendance at rugby training. The plans for the tour were well under way. Dixie and Ben had been given the task of organizing the post-match bar activities and were nominated as custodian of the 'fines' box. This was a converted ammunition box, which had been painted in the club colours of red and black and was destined to contain all the fines from players who will transgress any of the written or unwritten rules of the Panthers Rugby Club. Crimes would only attract cash fines, as no cheques were accepted. They included such heinous felonies as drinking with the wrong hand, being caught sleeping during bar open hours or leaving beer in your glass. The moneys from the box would be used, at the Captain's discretion to buy the beers, when appropriate. The custodian of the fines box was a prestige job and Dixie and Ben were really chuffed to be selected from a cast of several.

The Jengo, Bart Simpson, called Ben into his office a week before Easter. Ben sensed that Bart had been given the job by Burton to pass on the news of extra duties. Ben expected to be handed the news of extra duties over Easter. That would scupper their immanent tour plans. He was therefore mildly surprised to learn that no duties were forthcoming. His Jengo told him that the extra duties had not been awarded yet but they would follow later on. The rugby tour was all systems go. Ben thanked Jengo Simpson. At the time Ben was completely unaware that the Jengo had pulled a few favours to persuade the Sengo not to shaft them both over the Easter period.

When Ben told Dixie the good news, he took it in his usual nonchalant manner. He then declared, as only Dixie could, that he'd always known that they would be going on tour. He then added for good measure,

" And Bully-boy-Burton isn't going to stop us now!"
Ben smiled at his best mate's bravado. His mind wandered away from Dixie's outburst of contempt for their Sengo. Ben thought to himself that he even might be able to get home to see his brother while they were back in UK.

The Monday morning arrived, when the team was due to board the trooper to fly back to UK. The ferry strike was still firmly in force and it was very much touch and go that they got air transport for the tour. A stroke of fortune had permitted the team to get seats. One of the officers, who played in the team, had a brother who ran the Air Movements Section. Blood being thicker than the numerous requests and gratitude's offered by everyone else, who was angling for lift to UK, secured the seats home and back at the end of the week. The trooper aircraft's take-off was delayed for hours, due to baggage handlers at Luton staging a work to rule. They landed eventually at Luton that evening.

A large coach took them on the long journey to an Army barracks near Brecon. All along the route there was frequent evidence to show that the union-led strikes were taking their toll. Rubbish was piled up in some towns and villages and pickets encamped like gypsies outside factories and industrial sites along the route they travelled along. It was like a flashback to the winter of discontent of the late seventies.

There was scarcely time for a beer that night. However during the coach trip to Brecon most players had covertly consumed enough beer and alcohol to ensure a sound and undisturbed night's sleep. Early the following morning the slumbering sportsmen were rudely awaken by the Team Coach who arrived at the barrack block at 0700 hours. All the players were in a deep peaceful and alcohol induced sleep. By banging two dustbin lids together he attempted to raise his sleepy charges for the training session, which was scheduled to start within the hour. The first game was that same afternoon but no one was in the mood for training or for any sort of physical activity at all at that godforsaken time in the morning. The Coach eventually succeeded and training was duly attended and completed by all.

The game kicked off at 14.30 hours that afternoon. It was a hard game, as all games against Army teams usually were. Feldbruch emerged victors by a slim but important margin. Both the bruised and bloodied teams retired to the clubhouse for the social event that was as important, if not more important, than the game itself.

Everyone enjoyed the evening activities in the clubhouse. Much beer was consumed, songs were sung and friendships were forged, as the intense conflict on the field was forgotten amid the smoke and beer fumes of the bar. Dixie had added to the weight of the coffers in the fines box from the players, as the beery night progressed.

The following afternoon the team's transport headed down the Welsh valley roads towards the next venue. It was to be the main game of the tour. RAF Llantwit was a Maintenance Unit and had long been regarded as the bastion of RAF rugby. They had a renowned reputation for turning out high quality players, which first emerged in the halcyon days of Welsh rugby. Lately the introduction of a mainly civilian workforce had diminished the team's performance. However they would still be formidable opponents and the after-game activities were guaranteed to be memorable. That evening the boys hit the local pubs and most of the team travelled to the seaside town of Barry for beer and the obligatory throat-scorching curry. The team returned in the early hours, after they had been well fed and extremely well watered. Fortunately the Coach had organized only a light training session the next morning. This was kind to both their heads and digestive systems.

The game kicked off at 14.00 hrs in the presence of RAF Llantwit's Station Commander. In his youth he had played rugby for England. He still was a very keen fan of the game. Accompanying him was what appeared to be hundreds of noisy spectators. Dixie remarked that they must take their rugby seriously down at Llantwit. Ben confirmed that they did, however, he knew the real reason was that it gave the spectators an afternoon off work to watch the match.

Dixie and Ben had a very successful first half, but the game and its tactics were dominated by the Feldbruch's scum half, Frankie Fuller. He'd played an inspired first forty minutes and at the break Feldbruck were two tries and conversions to the good with Llantwit's only response being two well kicked penalties. The second half was a bruising and bad tempered affair. The Tourists managed to maintain their upper hand but several nasty incidents resulted in the occasional swapping of punches.

At the final whistle Feldbruch emerged victors by 17 points to 12.

As always the conflict seen on the field dissolved in the clubhouse. Llantwit's captain stood up in the bar and thanked the visitors for the hard-fought game and announced that a free barrel of beer had been put on for all to enjoy. Frankie Fuller was also named man of the match. He had to down a pint of beer, whilst standing on a chair and of course, as tradition demanded he was liberally doused with beer as he drank his ale. Of course he was also fined by Dixie for drinking his beer with the wrong hand.

The crowd in the clubhouse began to thin out around 9 pm. Most people were drunk out and completely sung out. Ben went off to find a phone to ring Wally to let him know that he might be able to pop home for a few hours at the end of the week, before heading back to Germany. Wally sounded in reasonable spirits. Ben was pleased, as he thought Wally had weathered the worse and was now on the mend.

Ben returned to the clubhouse. He found Dixie, who was stood near the bar and was clearly well under the influence. Dixie confidently announced that he was in urgent need of a curry. Ben knew it was his responsibility to make sure his best mate could obtain his much desired eastern delicacy. He also had to ensure that Dixie was also returned to his bunk in one piece. That's what the front row union demanded. They both got a taxi into Barry town centre and went in search of the same curry house they had eaten at the previous night. The vindaloo that they'd enjoyed so much the previous evening was a real bum-burner. Dixie declared in a loud vocal outburst, as he always did, when discussing the merits of curry:

" A good curry always burns twice - on the way in and on the way out, so bung the bog roll into the fridge for the morning." Dixie laughed, as he always did after reciting his well-practiced verse. However Ben had heard it so often before that he mouthed the words in time and in silence with Dixie's short monologue.

The two buddies stumbled down a side street in search of their goal. They turned a corner into a quiet side street. Ben had to steer his pal along the narrow pathway created by the temporary roadworks that extended along their side of the street. They had almost got to the end of the walkway, when they were approached by four teenagers. One of them shoulder barged into Dixie, whose unsteady legs buckled on the impact. Ben grabbed at Dixie's arm to stop him hitting the floor.

"Watch where you're going mate!" Ben shouted at the young lad.

The other three youths crowded round and the biggest of them pushed his face close up to Ben's. The beery and halitosis-laden breath that the youth expelled made Ben recoil slightly. The youth spoke in a menacing voice with the distinctive Cardiff accent.

"So who have we got here boys?"

One of the others added from a safe distance behind his obvious leader,

"I bet they're coppers; you can always tell by their feet and stupid looks."

Their leader chirped in again,

" Of course they're coppers, down from England on anti picket duties." He stared up and down Ben's imposing frame. He added, " Why don't you piss off back home and leave us alone?"

Dixie was now back on his feet and was beginning to get annoyed with his ungeniel Welsh hosts... He grabbed the collar of the nearest yobbo and yelled at him,

" We're not coppers we're servicemen ... so piss off yourselves". He added, "It must be past your bed time, so sod off home to yer Mammy, Taffy boyo."

Ben winced at the provocative words that Dixie blurted out. Suddenly two of the teenagers jumped on to Dixie and started laying into him. Ben didn't wait for an invite to come to the assistance of his buddy, so he punched the nearest yobbo to him. It sent the unguarded young lout sprawling over the road. Ben turned to help Dixie, who was loosing the battle against his three attackers. They were giving him a good kicking. Ben didn't like any one putting the boot in. He saw red at this. He dipped his shoulders and drove at the nearest unfriendly body. He crashed his target into the roadwork barriers. They had been positioned to ward off anyone from falling into the recently excavated hole. They didn't stop the battling pair from crashing to the bottom of the cavity. Ben quickly re-emerged from the crater. He left his opponent gasping for air in the depths of the hole. Ben then saw one of Dixie's attackers raising a steel road traffic sign above his head with the intention of pummeling Dixie with it. Ben sprung forward and rugby tackled the attacker from the side and for good measure he angled a punch into the groin of his opponent.

The traffic sign was immediately released. It missed its intended target but smashed through the glass window of the shop next to where Dixie was stood. The distinctive sound of breaking glass triggered the illumination of several lights from windows above the nearby shops. The burglar alarm from the now windowless shop added to the cacophony of sound. This was the cue for the local youths to run or try to run away from the scene. The poor victim from Ben's tackling limped and hobbled after his comrades. Dixie struggled to his feet, as Ben was carefully nursing his own swollen knuckles. Blood dripped onto the pavement from Dixie's broken nose; tentatively he fondled his injured proboscis. Looking at its misshapen reflection in what remained of the shop window he declared in exasperation:

" They've broken my bloody nose!" And added as an after-thought, "It's ruined me handsome good looks."

Ben was laughing at his mate's comments and did not notice the approaching police siren. Neither registered the imminent arrival of the police vehicle until the whole street was bathed in a pulsing umbrella of blue light. Ben was quickly confronted by a very large policeman. He manhandled Ben roughly and forced his right arm up his back. Ben and Dixie were both issued the mandatory caution, as they were quickly frog-marched towards the back of the waiting police van. After being bundled ungracefully into the back of the van, the doors were slammed shut behind them.

At the Barry police station Ben and Dixie tried to explain their version of the incident, which had led up to the window being smashed. But the Custody Sergeant played deaf, as he dutifully noted the contents of their pockets. His eyebrows rose as he found their RAF ID Cards. Before Dixie and Ben were placed in separate cells, they were charged with criminal damage to property.

They remained incarcerated for several hours, until a RAF Police Sergeant came to collect them. When they returned to RAF Llantwit, they thought they would be released and sent back to their beds. To their dismay they spent the rest of the night inside the guardroom's detention cell. The cell door was finally opened at 07.30 hours the next morning. Its two dishevelled occupants were paraded in front of the Duty Officer who peered down his bony nose with a look of disgust, passing some general comment about drunken rugby players. He signed the Occurrence Book as dictated by regulation and calmly chatted to the Duty Sergeant, until the arrival of the Flight Lieutenant Billy Garfield.

Billy Garfield was officer-in-charge of the Feldbruch Rugby Tour party. He was not best pleased with Dixie and Ben. As he walked with them back to the barrack block, he told them both to get cleaned up and report to back him in two hours time.

When Dixie and Ben, much cleaner and smelling far better, reported to Billy Garfield they had expected a bit of an ear bending and a major input towards the growing coffers in the fines box. They were both utterly stunned, when he delivered a bombshell of news. He explained that, somehow, the news of their arrest had reached Feldbruch. Both Dixie and Ben were to return back to Germany on the next available flight.

Ben was completely devastated. Not only would they miss the rest of the tour but it also meant that he wouldn't be able to go home as he had hoped to see his brother. A RAF Police car took both, the very dejected Ben and Dixie to Luton Airport, where they and a Police escort boarded the aircraft bound for Germany.

They landed back at RAF Feldbruch at 17.30 hours and were swiftly ushered through customs and driven straight to the guardroom and marched into the detention cells. About an hour later they were visited by Squadron Leader Burton. He gloated over the sight of his two corporals in the predicament they had landed themselves in. He hinted that the whole distasteful episode would be the final straw and court martial would be the likely outcome. Finally after making his feelings crystal clear, he announced that they would both be released from the guardroom. They would, however remain under open arrest. This meant they were restricted to camp and not to go into any of the bars on the unit and that part of the conditions of their release, Dixie found the hardest to stomach.

CHAPTER 7

Ben rang home to speak to Wally the day after he'd arrived back into Germany. Sarah answered the phone and she was close to tears. Ben explained to her that he would not be coming home as he had expected. He waffled on about being called back for work reasons and didn't mention the trouble he landed himself in during the tour. But Ben wanted to know why Sarah was crying. At first she wouldn't say but eventually she admitted that Wally had gone out to sell his shotguns. The strike, which Wally opposed so vehemently, had drained all their savings. They had been forced to sell off their things, bit by bit, to keep the mortgage payments up. Stunned by this news, Ben promised to send a cheque home for them but he knew that Wally was far too proud to cash it.

Ben went back into work on the squadron the next day. It then dawned on him the notoriety he had gained on the short but eventful rugby tour. His locker had been secretly opened and he found his overalls had been converted into a convict's uniform. Someone had adorned them with little black arrows, the window near his locker had vertical bars made from black sticky tape stuck onto the glass and a note pinned along side read,

" To Ben - to make you feel at home!" He knew no malice was intended. It was the usual serviceman's black humour that made light of adversity.

On the Friday the formal charges of, 'Conduct unbecoming an airman' had been processed by the Station Headquarters. Squadron Leader Burton's office door was firmly shut as Corporals Brownley and Dean stood outside awaiting an invitation inside for the charge to be read. Dressed in their best uniforms they were fully expecting the charge to be referred to the Wing Commander and then onto the Station Commander. Both had almost resigned themselves to the fact that a Court Marshall would, more than likely follow. The daunting prospects of a stint of penal servitude inside of Her Majesty's Military Detention Centre at Colchester, was a worrying reality. As they waited Warrant Officer O'Reilly came charging out of his office, barged through the Sengo's door without knocking and pulled it shut behind him. A few minutes later he re-emerged with a satisfying smile on his face. Ben caught the parting words of the Sengo as O'Really O'Reilly exited the door,

" I suppose you'd better tell them both. Thank you, Mr O'Reilly."

The Warrant Officer ushered Ben and Dixie into his office. He could not disguise how pleased he was, as he related his news to his two young subordinates. They stood speechless as it was explained that they were both admonished from all charges. The RAF Police had received information from the civilian police in Barry, South Wales, who revealed that their fight had been witnessed by an old man who lived nearby, and he had seen the whole incident. He also had experienced trouble from the same four youths and when he learnt that two airman were getting the blame for the damaged window, he came forward. Warrant Officer O'Reilly explained that the Police had no option but to drop the charges. Sengo Burton also had to agree, although it nearly choked him to admit it. O'Really O'Reilly knew his two Corporals were no angels but they were both hard working lads. However he didn't believe that they should be pilloried by Sengo for something of which they were innocent.

He dismissed Ben and Dixie but before they both left the office, he strongly advised them both to try and keep out of trouble and give the Sengo a wide berth for a day or so...at least until he had calmed down.

A few days passed with Ben managing to keep well out of the Sengo's way. He was concerned that again he had been unable to contact Wally. Every time he rang home, Wally was not in.

During the following week, a new list of duties was pinned up on the crewroom notice board. Ben wasn't surprised to see both his and Dixie's names nominated for Orderly Corporal duties over the early May Bank Holiday period. They had both expected it. Unfortunately for Ben, it would have been the next real opportunity for him to fly home to see his brother.

The British Forces in Germany received the UK news via the Services TV Channel. Ben wasn't normally a keen t.v. viewer but recently he had made a point of watching the news programmes. He often watched the news in utter disbelief, as it looked as if the country was being slowly strangled and held to ransom by the unions. The gutless government appeared to be powerless to stop the unions from destroying the fabric of society. There were video snippets on the news bulletins of how the strikes were effecting different parts of the country. One short report showed angry scenes outside a factory in Wales. Ben immediately recognized the mouthpiece of the Wrexham branch of the T&GWU. It was Keith Reece. He was addressing his union membership and was trotting out the usual verbal diarrhoea for the benefit of the TV reporters and cameras. It was vintage trade unionism of the seventies and to Ben it appeared that Wally was absolutely right and Reece was the key man behind all the union militancy in his local area.

Still worried about his brother, Ben was thankful that at least his own work had not been him causing any problems. Of course it had helped that the Sengo had been away on a training seminar. Dixie had continued to try and keep up the morale of his best mate and dragged him into the clubhouse at every opportunity.

The annual RAF Feldbruch Sevens Rugby Competition was held at the end of April. This pepped up Ben and helped to take his mind off things back at home. Feldbruch had a strong team and were expected to make it into the final at the very least. There were over thirty teams competing and the clubhouse bar did a roaring trade. The weather was ideal for rugby and, as expected, Feldbruch powered their way into the final. They had produced some outstanding running rugby that no other team seemed to have an answer too.

Just before the final game was due to kick off, Flight Lieutenant Bart Simpson turned up looking for Ben. He met him coming out of the changing rooms and he carefully guided Ben back inside as they moved into the Referee's room. Ben was puzzled about his Jengo's actions. He became even more concerned when the Padre turned up and closed the door behind him. Jengo Simpson had a serious expression on his face and this made Ben increasingly concerned and even more puzzled. Looking at both the officers, he spoke with a slight hint of panic in his voice,

" What's the matter? What's wrong? What's going on? Sir?"

Jengo Simpson looked at Ben; his fateful words left the young Corporal dumbstruck,

"I'm so sorry Ben, Your brother has been found dead. I'm afraid it looks like he took his own life."

Ben tried to mouth words to ask questions but nothing came out. He slumped into the chair behind him. A silence that seemed to last an eternity fell upon the small room.

Finally, Ben asked if he could go home as soon as possible. Jengo Simpson agreed of course and said that he would arrange the flight back to the UK for first thing the next day. The Padre offered his words of comfort, as he led Ben out of the door. As they emerged from the changing rooms, Dixie came bounding up and in his usual vivacious manner, he called out for Ben to get a grip and get down to the pitch. He never finished his request for Ben to join him on the pitch for the final game. He could see there was a problem by the look on Ben's face. It was etched with pain and shock. Jengo Simpson pulled Dixie to one side to explain what had happened, as the Padre steered Ben away from the clubhouse.

Dixie ran and caught up with Ben and the Padre as they approached the barrack block.

"It's OK Padre, I'll look after him from here" said Dixie.

The Padre patted Ben on the shoulder and left. Inside Ben's room the atmosphere was strange. They both sat on the bed and talked a little. At first Ben was very quiet, but slowly he started to speak and then it seemed as if he never was going to stop. To begin with Ben was upset but then he became angry. The months of anguish that had passed with Wally under the cosh of the unions had come to a tragic head. Ben was soon punching his pillow in anger and swore his hatred for the unions. He wanted revenge. Tears streamed down his face as he pummeled the pillow. Dixie knew that Ben needed to vent his emotion, so he let him get on with it.

The Wing Commander sent his own car round the following morning to pick up Ben from the barrack block. There was no scheduled trooper flight that day. Instead Bart Simpson had arranged a flight home by civilian aircraft. The Wing Commander's car was well on his way to Dussledorf Airport, before Ben had realized that he hadn't rang home to contact Sarah. In the circumstances and the shock of the news it had slipped Ben's mind. She must have been distraught Ben thought to himself. He tried to ring from the airport but it was Sarah's next-door neighbour who answered. Ben told her that he was on the way home and asked if she could let Sarah know.

The flight back to UK, although only an hour or so, seemed to last for ever. Ben kept seeing Wally's image in everything that he looked at. His anger welled up again and he began to blame himself for not being home with Wally, while he was struggling with the unions. He even blamed himself for missing the chance to see him, while he back in U.K. playing rugby. All these matters were whirling around his mind, as he left the airport arrivals lounge at Luton.

There were inevitable delays to the trains due to union strike action and by the time he finally boarded the train in London heading for North Wales, he was still turning the tragic loss of Wally over and over in his mind.

When the train finally pulled into Wrexham's General Station, it was 4:15 pm. Ben had to hail a taxi for the six-mile journey to Wally's house, as the buses were on strike again. When he arrived, Sarah was stood outside in the back garden. She was staring over the fence and down across the valley towards what was left of Brymbo Steelworks, where Wally used to work. She saw Ben and ran towards him and hugged him tightly, sobbing pitifully on his shoulder as her tears soaked into Ben's shirt. She turned and looked again towards the Steelworks,

"That's where they found him" she said choking back her tears, " He left this note on the mantelpiece. " Sarah held a small piece of paper in her hand. It was Wally's handwriting and in the green ink he always used for letters. She added, "He'd had enough, he couldn't take anymore so he drove down to the works, doused his car and himself in petrol and ...."

She didn't finish what she was saying as she burst into tears again. Ben held her in his arms for a moment and then steered her gently inside the house. They talked about Wally for hours to well past midnight. Ben was dog-tired but he felt Sarah needed to talk. It was a sort of therapy for her. They couldn't make any arrangements for the funeral, until the formalities had been observed. Sarah could not face the distressing task of formally identifying her husband's body, so Ben volunteered to do it for her.

The next morning Ben went down to the mortuary of the local hospital. He was joined by the local community policeman, PC Arthur Jenkins. He was there to see that formalities were observed and the paperwork was duly completed. Jenkins knew Wally quite well, as he had been doing regular checks over the years on the security arrangements for his shotguns. As they both waited to enter the viewing room, PC Jenkins explained the procedure to Ben. He confirmed that, under the circumstances, it wouldn't be necessary to identify the body as the effects of the fire had made that impossible and it often causes distress to relatives. However there were several personal effects taken from the body that could be used to verify identification. PC Jenkins also told Ben that he had seen Wally driving onto the site of the steelworks not twenty-five minutes before the fire was discovered by the site watchman. He'd assumed that Wally was visiting the site for nostalgic reasons, as many ex-steelworkers had recently. PC Jenkins also explained that he'd had the distressing task of breaking the tragic news to Sarah.

Inside the mortuary Ben was handed a wedding ring and a St Christopher necklace. Both had been badly distorted by the heat but the St Christopher medallion had Wally's initials on the back. The final item passed over was a Swiss army knife. Ben knew that Wally never went anywhere without it. Despite the red plastic side pieces fusing together with the blades and attachments, it was still easily recognizable. Ben showed PC Jenkins that the main blade had half an inch missing from the end, a result of Wally's over exuberance trying to prize open a locked cupboard door.

This was Wally's body and Ben was glad in a way that he did not have to see the badly disfigured remains of his brother.

After Ben had left the hospital, he went back to see Sarah to sort out the funeral details. She decided that a short service in the local chapel would be followed by a cremation. Ben knew that cremation was hardly necessary but he did not want to upset Sarah anymore by suggesting the alternative.

Sarah had been thinking hard about her future without Wally. She had already decided, however, that after the funeral, she would sell up the house and move away from the area completely. She would go to live with Uncle Percy who was a sheep farmer living near Caple Curig in the Snowdonia National Park. He had been made a widower last year; so Sarah would be able to look after him. The solitude of the farm, far away from the memories of the past year, would help her to come to terms with her loss. As much as Ben didn't like to see the family home sold off, he knew it was the right thing for her.

On the day of the funeral it was cold, wet and miserable. Held in the local Methodist Chapel, the service was simple and very moving. Ross Evans, the landlord from the Ty Inn, said a few well-chosen words about Wally but it was a great comfort for Sarah to see so many of her husband's friends at the service. The cremation that followed was for family and very close friends only. Ben was a tower of strength for his sister-in-law and he kept his composure right up to the point that the Vicar commended the body up and he signalled for the curtains to close around the coffin. At that exact instance a power cut put out the lights and silenced the organist who was playing Wally's favorite

Beatle's song, 'Let it be.' It was all just too much for Sarah, who slumped down in her pew sobbing. Ben thumped the front of his pew in anger and through his gritted teeth and sobs he protested,

" They've killed him. So why wont they just leave him in peace now?"
The timing of the power cut, which was due to the ongoing industrial action, was purely coincidental. However nothing could convince Ben that it wasn't the union hierarchy having a final stab at Wally for daring to stand up against their terror tactics. The sight of the undertakers pulling the curtain around the coffin was the final indignity for the Brownley family. Ben led Sarah outside. Both were in tears but Ben was incensed with hatred for the people responsible for his brother's death and undignified departure from this world.

After a few moments to compose themselves, they thanked the vicar for the service. Then the family and friends viewed the flowers that had been discreetly removed from the coffin and placed in a small garden near the crematorium. A well-dressed stranger, who was not at the service, came up to Ben and Sarah to offer his condolences. Everything was fine at first; Sarah smiled weakly at the kind words offered by the gentleman. But when he explained that he was the representative from the T&GWU, Ben just snapped. He lunged at the stranger but was prevented from inflicting the kind of harm he had intended by the strong arms of Ross Evans. He must have realized who the stranger was and positioned himself for just such an eventuality. Ross firmly and swiftly led the man away. Ben forgot he was in the Garden of Remembrance, as he vented his wrath against the union man with threats and insults. When he was spent of all his rage, he broke down and cried unashamedly.

The funeral tea was held in the Ty Inn, Wally's old watering hole. Ben had fully recovered his composure and was scurrying around making sure everyone had a drink. They all raised their glasses to Wally's memory. Just before Ben left the pub, he spoke to Ross and told him that somehow, sometime in the future he would avenge his brother's death. Ross could tell by the anger in Ben's eyes that he meant it.

Ben had to fly back to Germany the following day, as his leave was up. Sarah was happy that she had everything under control. The arrangements for the house sale were well in hand. Ben wanted to stay longer and ask for more leave but Sarah insisted that she could cope. Just before the taxi turned up to take Ben to the railway station in Wrexham, Sarah called him into the lounge. She was stood watching the BBC news. She said nothing but just pointed to the screen as Ben entered the room. The news reader read out a statement. It said that the government had finalized negotiations with the TUC as they had given some major concessions to the unions, but they had finally secured an end to the industrial action that had almost ruined the country. Ben was mortified and swore openly at the t.v. set. The outpouring of anger he had so publicly aired at the crematorium the day before erupted again. He remonstrated at the news reader who, of course, was oblivious to the effect his comments were having on Ben.

Eventually he started to calm down. Now, more than ever, he was convinced that the whole sorry, unnecessary mess had been created by the greedy unions and was the direct cause of the loss of his brother. Ben was still seething with anger, as he kissed Sarah good-bye and climbed into the taxi. During the long and boring journey back to Feldbruch, Ben racked his brain of how he could seek a suitable revenge for Wally's premature demise.

CHAPTER 8

Ben Brownley pulled tight on the laces of his trainers as he readied himself for a five-mile run with Dixie. He went outside the barrack block to stretch off his muscles, while he waited for his running partner to turn up. When Dixie arrived a few minutes later, they both jogged off together at a relaxed pace for the first couple of miles. The route they had chosen took them around the track that contoured the station perimeter fence. Most air bases occupied quite a large tract of land. Feldbruch was much bigger than most and a large proportion of it comprised a heavily-wooded, military training area. It was criss-crossed with tracks and roadways, which made it an absolute heaven for runners and joggers.

Ben and Dixie had covered just over three miles when they had to stop for a break. Ben was bursting for a pee. They decided to rest for a while at the inviting grassy glade alongside the track they'd been pursuing. The sun beamed down between the tall evergreen trees: it made an idyllic place to chill out a while. Laying on their backs, they both stared up at the clear blue sky. Ben shaded his eyes with his hands as he tracked a high-flying, four engined aircraft, as it headed westward towards UK and beyond. Dixie worked intently on splitting a long blade of grass. He held the blade to his lips and blew hard to try and generate a high pitched screech from it. He was, as always, unsuccessful in his futile attempt.

Ben chatted about his brother and the funeral. All the anger and hatred, he'd felt towards the unions, re-surfaced yet again. He told Dixie that he needed to avenge such an unnecessary death. He was, however, at a loss of how to achieve it. Dixie joked, as he usually did, when faced with an unfamiliar situation laughingly suggesting that Ben got somebody to shove a bomb up the arse of the TUC hierarchy. After a short pause he also added with a chuckle,

" Better still. Why not get one of our aircrew to drop a thousand pounder on their friggin' heads instead?"
Ben laughed, agreeing that it could definitely be a more suitable option and would make him feel better anyway. They both lay in silence for a minute or two as they simultaneously, thought of the spectacular results of such sweet revenge.

Ben suddenly turned his head on one side to look at Dixie. Slowly and deliberately he spoke to his best friend,

"Better still why not drop the bomb myself...and blow the bastards to bits? "

"Oh yes" replied Dixie in a quick-fire response," I can just see the Wingco lending you one of Her Majesties 20 million pound flying machines to nip over to UK and bomb the shit out of some bolshi union prats."
Ben's brow furrowed slightly revealing a hint of annoyance as he explained to Dixie that he was perfectly aware that he wouldn't be able to just 'borrow' an aircraft. Dixie waited intently and in silence for further elaboration from Ben. After a brief pause, Ben declared that he would simply have to steal one instead.

Dixie emitted a huge roar of laughter and clapped his hands together. He jumped to his feet and stared down at Ben.

"You must be pissed, Benny Boy. How the hell are you going to pull that one off?" Dixie asked amusingly of his mate.

"I don't know yet" replied Ben looking up, "But I'll work it out somehow, you just wait and see."

Ben then rose to his feet and placed his hand on Dixie's shoulder. With his eyes moistening, he looked straight at Dixie and poured out his heart to him. He described exactly how he'd felt, when he found out how his brother had died and how his brother had suffered. He knew now, that he just had to strike back at those responsible. He reminded Dixie that they went back a long way and they'd always stuck together - through thick and thin. Ben also recalled that Dixie had promised to help him to get justice for Wally's death.

Dixie did not reply straight away. His head was bowed and he carefully studied his feet. But he then slowly looked up, smiled at Ben, winked his right eye and replied:

"Why not? Benny Boy, Why not? After all, neither of us seem to have much of a long-term future in this man's Air Force... so lets go out with a bang! "

They both started to walk down the track back towards the barrack block, chatting as they walked. They discussed how they could possibly steal an aircraft, but none of their initial ideas made sense or were remotely feasible. They started to jog gently, still exploring options. Some were outrageous, some impracticable but still nothing seemed anyway credible. The jog soon turned into a trot, then into a run, as the barrack block came into sight, they raced each other to the door. They arrived at the door neck and neck. As they each fought to recover their breath they agreed, for the moment, not to discuss their plans any further. They would talk about it the next time they went for a run; that way they would not be overheard.

The next day Dixie, dressed in his running kit, rapped loudly on Ben's door. They had arranged to go for another five miler. There was no answer. After several minutes of waiting, Dixie left and went on the run on his own. Ben had planned to go with Dixie but his attention was otherwise occupied in the Station library at the time he should have been out running.

He had lain awake most of the previous night, as he juggled with options of what to do and how to actually steal an aircraft. The minute he woke in the morning, he was back in thinking mode. As he lay staring at the ceiling a thought came to him. He realized he would have to hit hard at the TUC hierarchy, and what better time to do so, than during the highly publicised annual conference. Ben was normally a mild-manner character, with the exception of his performance on the rugby pitch of course. Now, however, he was contemplating killing a whole assembly of union officials and its members. It frightened him but the overwhelming desire for revenge overruled his temporary fear. He needed to find out when and where the conference would convene. He knew that it would be sometime in September or October.

Ben dressed quickly and set off for the station library to 'surf' the universal font of all knowledge, the Internet. Time passed quickly and Ben missed his running appointment with Dixie, as he ploughed his way around the TUC's web site.

It was full of useless information but it did give the dates of the conference, which was scheduled for the second week in September. Ben couldn't believe his luck when he saw the location. It was to be held at the Pier Conference Centre, Llandudno.

This was a place Ben knew very well. He had visited there many times as a young boy. All that area of North Wales was familiar to him as Wally used to drive the family around Snowdonia on weekends he wasn't on shift at the Steelworks. Ben started to formulate the outline of a plan. Now, armed with his target location and date, he left the library. He had a noticeable bounce in his step, as he headed back to the barrack block to tell Dixie. Suddenly Ben stopped in his tracks and checked his watch,

"Oh sod it!" he said to himself, as he realized he should have been out running with Dixie. He quickened his pace and, as he turned the corner near the barrack block, he saw Dixie, who was stretching off his muscles after his run. Dixie spoke through gasping intakes of air, as he recovered his breath,

"So you finally... turned up. Pity you missed the last.... five miles."

Ben replied with a little embarrassment,

"Sorry mate but come inside, we need to talk."

Inside Ben's room they both sat down on the bed. Dixie gulped back the entire contents of a litre bottle of water that he'd taken from Ben's fridge in the corner of the room. Ben explained what he'd found out from the Internet and he seemed very pleased with his news. However for the moment he didn't want to tell Dixie the entire plan that he'd already cooked up in his head. Dixie reached for another bottle of water as he sweated profusely now he was inside of Ben's room. He turned to look at Ben, who had walked over to the window,

"There's only one thing wrong with your plan Benny Boy" Dixie replied with a grin. He then added, "You do realize that the second week in September is also the Taceval exercise week."

Dixie spun round and yanked open his locker door. On the inside was the year planner he'd 'acquired' from the squadron admin clerk. His finger traced along the month of September and there in red ink was the word 'Taceval', spread over the Wednesday to Friday of that second week.

"Bollocks" exclaimed Ben, slapping the door with the open palm of his right hand.

Dixie spoke as he pulled off his Nike trainer and sock to examine the sole of his left foot.

"So what's Plan B then, Benny Boy?"

Dixie waited for a response. He then confessed that he did at one time; believe that his best mate might be able to pull off his daring stunt... providing he could actually fly the aircraft of course. But to try and steal one, when the squadron was fully manned and at a high state of alertness, was a definite none starter. Ben was staring intensely at the month of September. He reached across to Dixie, pulling on his arm, without taking his eyes off the planner on the back of the locker door.

"No Dixie, take a look at this" Ben said with renewed excitement.

They scrutinized the planner together, as Ben's finger underlined the entries he had placed against that week. It showed against the weekend before Taceval that he'd written in felt tip pen 'Working Week-end?' Ben had put that in as everyone had fully expected the Sengo to insist on the squadron working to ensure the aircraft were ready for such a major exercise. Then Ben jabbed his finger at Monday and Tuesday of the week...for the benefit of Dixie.

"See, Monday is a normal working day but Tuesday is a German Public Holiday" Ben added with growing excitement. Dixie looked puzzled. He couldn't see the significance. Ben explained slowly to his obviously confused mate.

" On Monday we will be doing the final prep for the exercise. And of course the Armourers will be bombing up the aircraft, because that's what the Sengo said we will do. And the Tuesday is a German public holiday."

Dixie still couldn't quiet comprehend what his oppo was driving at. Ben continued.

" Look! You know that there will be no flying on Tuesday and it'll be a station stand-down. So we'll volunteer to look after the squadron on that day when every one else is off. And then we'll be able to nick the jet."

"As simple as that" added Dixie somewhat sarcastically.

Ben was getting a little annoyed with Dixie. But he continued to explain even though he had not yet fully finalized every detail in his own mind. However he did acknowledge that flying the aircraft was the one big problem he had yet to overcome. Nevertheless he'd convinced Dixie into agreeing that they would plug at it together and they had almost five months to sort out the problem. Dixie then left Ben's, room still trying to comprehend exactly what Ben had in mind, as they both needed to get ready for night shift.

The next few days passed quickly. They didn't discuss the plan any further, because they were too busy at work and had no time for running. The early May bank holiday was approaching, so they would have plenty of time off to get some decent runs in and also plenty of chances to chat about and develop their plan.

The first day of the bank holiday Dixie was on duty in the Guard Room as Orderly Corporal. While Dixie was on duty, Ben decided to grab an early morning run. He set off to cover the short distance to the place, where he and Dixie stopped over during their last run together.

Ben pushed his own pace hard to reach the glade as soon as he could. He didn't know whether it was an earnest desire to improve his fitness or just to enable him to get down to some serious thinking and planning as soon as possible. That shaded, grassy location seemed to generate inspiration when it came to masterminding his plot. Ben was panting hard when he arrived at the sunlit clearing in the trees. He collapsed onto his back in the luscious green vegetation; his chest heaved up and down as he struggled to overcome the temporary lack of oxygen in his blood.

Slowly Ben recovered by inhaling large quantities of fresh, clean air into his lungs. He found himself again, prostrate on his back, his eyes scanning the cloudless sky, like the last time he'd visited the clearing. Looking up, Ben saw a four-engined airliner cruising the stratosphere. A few minutes later he saw another but this one was not flying quite so high. In the twenty minutes or so that he had been at the clearing, Ben's pulse and respiration had almost returned back to normal. During that time, he'd seen several aircraft crossing left to right, traversing the relatively small segment of sky that was visible from the tree-encompassed clearing. This made Ben think. He knew that civil airlines were allocated specific air routes in the sky. They were like the motorways of the air. If any of the aircraft that Ben had seen were destined for UK, he might be able to use those routes to help him execute his plan. Ben knew he would have to wait until after the holiday, before he could check his facts back at the squadron.

Ben jogged back to his room with another possible piece of his plan slotted into place. With Dixie on duty overnight, Ben passed his evening by sitting in a deck chair outside the barrack block with a few beers. He surveyed the evening sky using his binoculars until it became too dark to see. Ben timed the frequency of west-bound aircraft as they powered their way through the evening sky. Some of them left the tell-tale white finger of a contrail from each of their engines but some only indicated their presences, when the rapidly descending sun reflected off their polished airframe or glass surfaces. They seemed to pass over at a rate of one every five or six minutes. Ben made a mental note of that timing.

The next morning Cpl Ben Brownley officially took over duty from Cpl Dixie Dean in the Guard Room. The duty of Orderly Cpl was one repeated daily on every RAF Station, wherever it was located. RAF Feldbruch's duty required the Orderly Corporal to man the phones, lock-up communal buildings and be general dogs-body, when the normal guardroom staff where not present.

Dixie's day had been uneventful. He told Ben that he might see him that evening in the NAAFI. There was a disco planned and he had a Vision of Loveliness lined up. That was Dixie's term for a pretty, accommodating young female.

Ben's day seemed to go on forever and, like Dixie, he also had a very quiet days duty. However before he could turn in for the night, he had to ensure the NAAFI was empty of all personnel and secured. This was the worse part of the Orderly Corporal's duties. It normally required considerable diplomatic skills to put up with the drunken ranting of late night drinkers who insisted in remaining ensconced in the NAAFI bars. The last thing anyone wanted was to call in the RAF Police as they usually arrested everyone, which meant endless paperwork and major inconvenience for Orderly Corporal.

Ben did manage, however, to empty the bar by quarter past midnight and as a result he was feeling pleased with himself. Finally he just had to check all the rest of the rooms in the NAAFI complex to ensure they were unoccupied. As he walked down the short corridor towards the snooker room he could hear voices and laughter from behind the door. He pushed open the door and he peered inside. The room was in darkness except for the snooker table light, which lit up the vivid green baize. The silhouette of a man stood at one end of the table with his back towards him. It prompted Ben to turn on the main lights of the room. Its sudden and total illumination, made the shadowy figures near the table respond,

"Do you bloody mind. Can't you see I'm busy?" snapped the anonymous stranger without looking in Ben's direction; his backside thrusting rhythmically against the end of the table. When Cpl Brownley's eyes eventually recovered from the blast of light, the body of the stranger appeared to have a pair of shapely female legs wrapped around his backside. One of the body-less legs had a pair of white silken panties hooked over its foot. The flimsy undergarments bounced about in time with the thrusting from the male's buttocks. A set of immaculately, manicured red fingernails were visible. They were trying to penetrate the shirt that covered the body of the man and exaggerated moans were emitted from the hidden female form.

Ben coughed and somewhat embarrassed, explained that he had to lock up the NAAFI. The face of the stranger turned towards him. It came as a bit of a shock to Ben, as he recognized it was the face of Mick Cookson, the Chief Technician who ran the Tornado Flight Simulator. Ben had met him previously, when he went to use the simulator to practice engine fire drills. Cookson was more than a little put out to be interrupted during his passionate interlude. As he was protesting in the finest Anglo Saxon expletives to the poor hapless Corporal, the female recipient of his amorous attentions popped her head around Mick Cookson's large frame.

Ben was stunned to see the pretty features of Samantha Burton. She smiled at Ben and inquired in her sultry voice,

" Corporal Brownley you are determined to spoil all of my fun. Aren't you?"

Chief Technician Cookson was surprised to hear that the young lady, to whom he was offering a portion of horizontal pleasure, was an acquaintance of the Orderly Corporal. Ben was a little shocked at what he had stumbled upon but he confirmed to Cookson that, yes he did know young Samantha. But composing himself he also added that he knew who her Dad was and how old she was. So, when Cookson heard that she was only fifteen and the daughter of a Squadron Leader, he swiftly disengaged himself from her entwining body. He was visibly shocked. His passion neatly and instantly truncated.

As all three walked back down the corridor towards the main exit. Samantha blew a goodnight kiss to Ben as she stuffed her panties into her handbag. She didn't even look at Mick Cookson, as she left the building.

Cpl Brownley was struggling to secure the main door to the NAAFI complex. The very worried chief technician was hovering at Ben's elbow. He was trying to find out if he was going to report what he had witnessed in the snooker room. Ben soon became a little impatient with the snivelling overtures from Mick Cookson. Ben didn't want to get drawn, at that precise time, on what he would be doing about his discovery. This antagonized Cookson, who changed tack and started to threaten Ben. Ben ignored him. Then, in desperation, Cookson offered a large cash inducement to purchase Ben's silence. Cpl Brownley, again without responding to Cookson, finally managed to lock up the main doors of he NAAFI. In silence he left alone to walk back to the guardroom.

Chief Technician Cookson was left to contemplate his illegal actions with a young girl, who was nearly the same age as his own daughter.

CHAPTER 9

Corporal Brownley climbed into his bed just before eight a.m. after completing his overnight duties in the guardroom. Despite being dog tired, due to being woken several times during the night to answer the phone, he couldn't get off to sleep. He kept seeing images of young Samantha peering around Cookson's shoulder, as he tried to quench his thirst for lust. However Ben knew that somehow he could turn his surprise discovery to his advantage. It than dawned on him that Mick Cookson could help him to get some very useful Tornado simulator training. Ben could therefore, learn the basics of flying the aircraft in safety and, hopefully, in relative secrecy. Blackmail was always referred to in films or on t.v. as a dirty word. Ben regarded it as most opportune in his case as he would merely have to suggest to Cookson that it would be in his best interest to comply with an apparently innocent request for a trip in the simulator. Contented with his successful early morning scheming, Ben turned over and then, with very little effort, tumbled into a most welcomed deep sleep.

Ben was dreaming. He was just about to drive off in a Ferrari with a busty, leggy blond in the seat alongside, when Dixie, banging on his room door, rudely wakened him. Ben staggered to the door to be met by a smiling Dixie, dressed in his tracksuit.

"Come on, Benny Boy, What d'ye know? What d'ye say"? piped Dixie in his usual effervescent manner.

Ben groaned. He turned away, pulling the door open to silently invite Dixie inside. He went to his fridge for a cold drink for himself and he gestured to Dixie with a tin of coke. Dixie waved away the offer. Instead, he reached inside Ben's sports bag, which was in its usual place under the bed and pulled out a well-worn rugby shirt and threw it across the room at his sleepy mate. Ben had just quaffed the last dregs of the orange juice from a carton when the flying shirt wrapped itself around his head. Pulling off the shirt, he let it fall to the floor and tossed the carton into the small bin by the door.

"Why are you so bloody cheery today and where were you last night?" Ben asked as he recovered from the abrupt reveille. Dixie replied:

" Well Benny Boy, it just happens to be my birthday today and I got laid last night. So we are going to give the run a miss today and go for a session of touch rugby with the boys and have a beer or two."

Ben, now fully equipped with his faculties, began to comprehend Dixie's intentions.

"But Dixie" added Ben, " I need to tell you about Mick Cookson and what he was up to last night with Sammy Burton."

" OK" said Dixie, "Get dressed and tell me on the way down to the club."

They both jogged across the lush green grass of the rugby pitch, tossing a ball between each other. A dozen or so other players were milling about inside the clubhouse. Ben had just finished explaining the events of the previous night as they reached the clubhouse door.

"What a dirty old pervert Mick Cookson turned out to be" said Dixie, almost shouting.

"Keep it down, Dixie, you dick-head. I need to keep that under wraps if we can make any use of it." Ben retorted.

Dixie shrugged his shoulders and pulled an imaginary zip across his mouth. Neither said any more in the presence of the rest of the players. They knew that the subject was closed until they were alone together again.

All the players were soon sweating hard, as they played touch rugby for over an hour or so. As it was the close season for the game, only training like touch rugby was authorized by the Ruby Football Union. It was supposed to be none contact and therefore less likely to cause injury. In practice it often wasn't quite the case. Ben slowly rose to his feet after running in his second try. As he turned to recover back to his own half of the pitch when he recognized the figure who was practicing his golf swing over on the adjacent soccer pitch. It was Chief Technician Cookson. Ben left the game temporarily, picking up a water bottle as he walked over to him.

" Hello Cpl Brownley...it's Ben Brownley isn't it?" Cookson inquired. Ben nodded in agreement and opened his conversation.

" Chief or can I call you Mick? About last night. You needn't worry, I'll say nothing of what I saw." The relief on Cookson's face was obvious as he burst into a nervous smile. He reached across to shake Ben's hand.

" Thanks Ben. You know, if there is anything I can do for you, just ask." replied Cookson with an almost embarrassing patronizing tone to his voice. Ben waited a few seconds before delivering his punch line.

" Since you asked... there is." he replied, " Any chance of a trip in your simulator? I know it's a busy place but I'm sure you can slip me in somewhere...in the evening maybe?" Ben stood in silence awaiting Cookson's response.

" No problem. Come and see me tomorrow night about eight o'clock. " Cookson added with relief coupled with a trace of bravado in his voice.

Ben turned and jogged back across field to the clubhouse just as Dixie was emerging from the doorway armed with two bottles of beer to quench their thirst. As Ben reached for the liquid refreshment on offer, Dixie guided him away from the rest of the crowd.

" What did old randy Cookson say to you?" asked Dixie.

" Not much... but I've wangled a trip in the Simulator in exchange for keeping quiet about his amorous adventures." Ben then explained that for the first trip he would go alone. Then he would introduce his navigator, in the guise of Dixie of course, a little later on. Dixie could now see Ben's plan and how he might be able to gain enough flying experience to pull off their outrageous act of revenge. They both returned to the bar and spoke no more about Cookson but concentrated on celebrating Dixie's birthday.

The next morning they returned to work as the short holiday was over. They both cycled down to the squadron dispersal, clearing their hangovers as they peddled. As soon as Ben had the opportunity, he went into the squadron flight-planning room. He needed to examine the large air chart that was mounted, under Perspex, on the wall. Just as Ben had hoped, it showed there were air lanes that traversed Western

Europe, it showed that they passed over the top of Feldbruch and led directly into UK air space. That was the route he would take and it would provide the perfect cover to permit, Dixie and him and their stolen aircraft to transit over to the east coast of Lincolnshire. From there on, Ben had yet to decide where he would go but clearly the plan was looking more and more feasible each day.

Ben couldn't wait to finish his day's work. He cycled energetically back to the barrack block with Dixie. As they rode, he told him of his discovery and the air routes they could use to fly over to the UK. Dixie was pleased to hear the news but he seemed a little bewildered at the pace with which Ben was driving events.

Later that evening Ben walked over to the Tornado Flight Simulator building. It was a green painted prefabricated steel construction with no windows; its air conditioning unit outlet on the roof droned away to itself. Ben was met at the main air-lock door by Mick Cookson, who smiled pleasantly at his guest.

" Come on in Ben. I've set the kit up for you. The cockpit's free for an hour, so you can enjoy yourself" Cookson explained to his guest.

Of course Ben had been inside the building before. He'd often sat in the cockpit, when practicing the mandatory emergency fire drills for ground testing of the engines, but he'd never managed to actually fly the simulator because Chief Technician Cookson was vehemently against groundcrew using valuable and unnecessary rig time. The main rig room contained a replica of the front fuselage of the Tornado aircraft mounted on a platform that could be moved and tilted by computer- controlled hydraulic rams. This gave the feeling of the motion that was experienced when flying.

Ben climbed into the front cockpit and pulled hard on the tight-fitting aircrew helmet, which isolated him from all outside noise. Only when he turned on the intercom was the stony silence broken. Mick Cookson's voice talked Ben through the pre-flight checks. As the cockpit layout was exactly the same as the real aircraft, Ben didn't need any help to start the engines, power up the flying controls or the air conditioning system. He had done all this during the numerous engine ground tests he'd done in his time. The canopy, which on simulators was normally painted white inside, closed shut with a thudding clunk. Ben's external vision was limited to the forward view out of the front windscreen. Its clear glass revealed a large screen with a computer-generated image of the runway projected on to it. In preparation for this moment Ben had read up the take off procedure in the aircrew manual he had 'borrowed' from the Sqn's library. He eagerly pushed the throttles forward and into afterburner and the cockpit gauges responded just as they would during engine testing for real. He let the brakes off as the engines passed through 50% afterburner and the cockpit dipped forward slightly. Suddenly the runway lights started to pass either side of the windscreen and the broad painted white centre line was gobbled up, disappearing under the nose of the aircraft as the air speed indicator confirmed his rapid acceleration.

The computer-controlled movements of the cockpit were synchronized with every movement of the control column and throttle. Ben felt the cockpit bounce and shake slightly. This made him feel, as if he was hurtling down the runway for real. As the aircraft lifted into the air, as if by itself, it passed through the computer-generated clouds. Ben's senses easily fooled his brain to believe he was actually flying and not tethered to the ground.

For the first few minutes his control movements were very erratic. He over-compensated for every adjustment he made, which was required to keep the aircraft level and on the same heading. Ben began to relax and soon was handling the aircraft with confidence and reasonable aplomb. The intercom broke his concentration. It was Mick Cookson's voice:

" Not a bad take off, but it might help if you raised your undercarriage before you reach 250 knots or you'll rip them off if you were really flying!" Ben looked down at the undercarriage selection lever. It was selected to down. He swore to himself but it was a simple enough error to make. After all he would never operate that under-carriage lever on the ground and he made a mental note not to forget it again in the future.

Ben flew around for half an hour trying different heights, speeds and manoeuvers. Mick Cookson remotely engaged the navigation system from the control console and gave Ben a basic route to follow. It brought him back heading towards the runway and Mick suggested that he tried to attempt a landing. Mick Cookson then talked him through the various cockpit checks and selections in preparation to land the aircraft.

" Wings to fully forward position. Flaps to fully down. Undercarriage selected down." Mick rattled out a fusillade of checks for Ben to follow, who'd then verbally confirm his selection when he had complied. Ben was concentrating hard on steering the aircraft down the centre line of the runway and descending at the correct rate. Suddenly the aircraft veered to the right, due to the simulated cross-wind inputted by Cookson from the control console. Ben wasn't expecting it and he looked anxiously down at the instrument panel. He yanked hard at the control column in an attempt to regain the correct heading. The aircraft responded to Ben's sudden and massive input to the flying controls and the aircraft leaped across the centre line over to the left. Ben gripped tight on the control column in his eagerness to regain directional control. But he'd completely forgotten to watch his height and rate of decent. When he finally looked up and out of the windscreen, he could see the runway coming rapidly up at him. His instincts made him slam both throttles forward in an attempt to add engine thrust and regain height. Warning horns were warbling loudly in his earphones and lights flashed from the instrument panel, the cockpit jerked violently and the screen picture suddenly went blank!

Mick Cookson spoke from the control console into Ben's earphones as he switched on the rig room lighting.

"Sorry Ben. You've crashed. But it wasn't a bad flight up to the point you attempted the landing."

Ben climbed out of the cockpit. He was soaking wet from perspiration. He smiled at Mick Cookson and admitted that he thoroughly enjoyed the experience. As he approached the exit of the facility, he broached the subject of another trip the next night and with Dixie, his mate, in the rear cockpit. Mick Cookson was not that happy about the request but finally agreed but he stated that it would have to be definitely a one off. Ben smiled to himself as he walked out of the building. He would tighten his hold over Cookson the next day, when he would reveal his plans for many more simulator sorties.

The next evening Ben and Dixie turned up at the simulator. They were met by Mick Cookson, whose facial expression clearly gave away the fact that he was less than over-joyed at hosting his two visitors. As Dixie was selecting one of the spare helmets and setting up the back cockpit, Cookson pulled Ben over to one side.

" Look Ben! You do realize that this will be the last trip I can let you have?" said Cookson, who seemed to be a little agitated with the situation.

Looking intensely at Mick Cookson, Ben replied with a smile like a stiletto bladed knife,

" Sorry Mick but I feel you just don't understand the gravity of your predicament. You know what I witnessed. It could rapidly end both your career and marriage... if it got out, of course. "

Cookson went pale and translucent beads of sweat appeared on his upper lip. Ben stepped closer to Cookson and, with a slightly menacing tone to his voice, he added:

" I'll promise to keep my mouth shut providing, that I can come down here now and again to get in some flying. I promise that I won't come when you're busy. So now, do we understand each other?"

Cookson swallowed hard at what he heard and tried to respond. He only managed to get the word "But" out of his mouth, when Ben interrupted him.

" I've also spoken to young Samantha. She said that she felt very embarrassed at what happened and if it got out she would say that you forced yourself on her." Ben knew that he was fabricating that part of the story but he also knew that Cookson wouldn't challenge it. And for good measure Ben added:

" Also, If it ever came out or you were stupid enough to go to your Boss about our little arrangement. I would say that I was only doing what poor, helpless little Samantha had asked me to do by keeping it quiet to save her shame and embarrassment."

Cookson was stunned into complete silence. The sweat on his upper lip was flowing like tap water so much so that he had to mop it up with his handkerchief. Dixie appeared from the other room. He had been behind the door listening to what Ben had been saying to Cookson. Even he was surprised to learn to what depth Ben would go to force through his plan. He broke the short silence that had prevailed between Ben and Mick Cookson,

" Are we going flying or what?" Dixie said with an obvious eagerness.

Ben nodded and steered Dixie towards the rig room.

They climbed into their respective cockpits and quickly ran through the pre-take off checks and were soon airborne and flying out towards the North Sea. With Dixie operating the radar and navigation kit from the back seat, it made a terrific difference to what they could simulate. The simulator, like the real aircraft, had a moving map display in both cockpits. It provided both the crew members with a display that showed a map, which could be selected to various scales, of the area below the aircraft. The radar image could overlay the map. This was a very useful and flexible system of navigation.

Ben and Dixie flew over to the UK coast and simulated a low level attack against Skegness pier. Ben had never liked the pier and it did provide some practice for the real target they would be eventually attacking. They flew around for a while over the North Sea and along the Dutch coastline. Ben followed navigational instructions from Dixie, who was thoroughly enjoying putting all his vast experience of the avionics kit into practice. Ben finally decided that it was time to return to base and to attempt a landing again. Dixie provided the route and Ben went through the checks as he approached the runway. It could be seen in the distance on the computer screen out of the front windscreen.

Mick Cookson was still reeling from the conversation that he'd had with Ben. So he was too pre-occupied with his thoughts to get involved with the sortie from the control console. Ben flew down towards the runway, this time there was no cross-wind. Mick Cookson's mind was elsewhere and he simply had not bothered to select any.

Ben concentrated harder this time to keep the aircraft on the correct heading. Dixie was calling out the altitude reading to aid Ben's task as the aircraft kept as steady as a rock as it descended down the glide-path. Waiting in anticipation, as the aircraft sunk down the last few feet to the runway, Ben was feeling very pleased with his second attempt at landing. Suddenly, the warning lights flashed and horns sounded in their earphones. Ben rapidly scanned the instrument panel and his natural instincts guided his eyes initially towards the engine gauges. He saw nothing amiss. He switched his attention towards the central warning panel; again nothing indicated what was wrong. Suddenly the cockpit lurched violently and the screen went blank again.

No input or explanation came from Cookson, who was still contemplating his dire predicament. Instead, Dixie shouted out,

" What the hell's happened?" Ben scanned the cockpit for some explanation. He then saw why the landing had ended in a juddering crash.

" Shit" Ben exclaimed in frustration. He hadn't selected the undercarriage down for the landing. Ben confessed his cock-up to Dixie, as they clambered out of their cockpits. Dixie joked with his budding pilot and hoped that he could master that element of flying before too long. Despite the unsuccessful landing, they had both fully enjoyed the flight.

Mick Cookson approached them both, as they exited the cockpit rig room. He was still in a state of shock but he now seemed to realize he was in a corner and he had no answer to the problem. He told Ben that if he wanted to come again, he would have to wait a couple of days, as the simulator was already booked up for aircrew. Ben explained that he did understand that they would have to fit in with the legitimate use of the simulator, but they would be back. Cookson was clearly not impressed by Ben's sudden considerate manner. Ben smiled at him as he patted him on his shoulder. Ben escorted Dixie out of the building and over to the club to celebrate with a beer or two.

CHAPTER 10

Ben and Dixie were very busy at work on the squadron throughout the months of June and July. Despite their heavy work-load, they still managed to accumulate over thirty hours flying in the simulator. That was more than most of the squadron aircrew flew each month themselves. Chief Technician Mick Cookson was not pleased with the arrangement that had been forced upon him. However working a few hours overtime to ensure that the rig was available for Ben and Dixie was viewed by him, as a small price to pay, when compared with the possible loss of both career and marriage.

Ben became reasonably competent at the rudiments of flying the Tornado aircraft. He had not managed to master the art of landing but Ben wasn't worried about that.... yet! They would often fly during the evening when they were on day shift, or they would pop into the simulator, if it was free, during their supper break during their night shifts.

They both realized that just flying the simulator would never be sufficient to equip them for the task they had planned. So Ben would sit and chat to the pilots whenever he could and discreetly quiz them about the performance parameters of the aircraft and how they would handle certain flying condition. Most of the young pilots were only too pleased to disgorge their knowledge of the aircraft. One of the more senior pilots asked why a mere corporal was so interested in the performance of the aircraft. Ben replied that he was studying aerodynamics for an Open University degree and that seemed to pacify him. Dixie was engaged in a similar mission and milked the combined knowledge of the junior navigators at every opportunity.

During the weekend the simulator was not available for their use. It would have been very difficult for Mick Cookson to explain to his boss the extensive use of the rig over Saturday and Sunday. Ben accepted this fact and Mick Cookson was highly relieved that his two ground-bound aircrew did not insist on weekend flying.

Ben and Dixie were kept busy with other activities. They put in quite a few miles running every weekend, so much in fact that Frankie Fuller inquired why they were training so much. Dixie replied that Ben and he were planning to run a marathon for charity. Frankie was keen to do the same so he asked if he could tag along with them. This genuine request was met with a short, sharp, negative rebuff from Ben. Dixie tried to calm the situation down by explaining to Frankie:

"Sorry Frankie, it's no use us two plodding, front-row donkeys trying to keep pace with a racing snake like you. You'd be better off running with one of the other lads. You understand don't you? "

Frankie Fuller nodded in agreement and left Ben and Dixie to go on their run together.

As they both jogged around the well-trodden route that they had been following for many months, Dixie spoke to Ben.

" Benny Boy, You were a bit sharp with Frankie back there. You'll have to lighten up or someone is going to suspect something's going on. "

Ben confessed that he knew that Dixie was right and replied:

"I'll sort myself out, Dixie, I promise. You know the plans were coming together but there's always some little detail that needs ironing out and I can do without the likes of Frankie Fuller interfering."

They both ran on in silence until they reached the glade where they normally stopped; by then it was raining lightly. They sat together and sheltered under a tree. Ben revealed to Dixie his latest thoughts of what they needed to do after they had completed the mission and successfully bombed the target. They both clearly understood that the RAF and the civilian police would be searching for them. Landing the aircraft anywhere in the UK was definitely not a viable option and ejecting out of the aircraft was their only choice. Both of them had completed a sports parachuting course a year or two before, so dropping out of the sky voluntarily did not hold much fear for either of them. Ben then elaborated for the benefit of Dixie on his initial thoughts of what they would need to do during the escape leg of the mission.

"After we hit the target, you'll have to give me a heading to get us over Snowdonia. We'll eject and let the aircraft crash into the mountains."

"And where do we go from there once we hit the ground?" asked Dixie.

Ben drew a rough sketch with a twig in the soil in front of them, as he explained,

" Look, we need to bang out somewhere south of the Capel Curig area. You know we're both pretty experienced at hill-walking, so we can make our way to my Uncle Percy's Farm on foot."

Dixie was a little surprised at the detail Ben had already worked out. He turned to Ben and inquired,

" But what will your uncle say, when we both pitch up unannounced?"

Ben smiled as he replied to his mate:

" That'll not be a problem, because we will be in the summer farm house and not at the winter farm house."

Dixie looked puzzled at the answer, which Ben gave. After a few seconds he asked,

"Sorry, Benny Boy but you'll have to translate that one for me."

Ben explained to Dixie that Uncle Percy still followed the old Welsh Hill farming traditions. In years gone by, all hill farms had two farmhouses. One was called the Hafod, which was the farm located high up the mountain hillside where the sheep could graze throughout the summer months. The second was called the Hendre. That farmhouse was down at the lower level of the valley, where the sheep were kept through the winter months for lambing. Ben knew that Uncle Percy would be in the Hendre in September. The Hafod would therefore be empty and it would be secure until the spring. Ben also knew where the spare key was hidden, as he had visited there several times with Wally. The upper farm had electricity and propane gas for heating and it always had food in the cupboards... for emergencies.

" The perfect hideout for a few weeks, until the heat goes down " Dixie added before Ben could.

Ben smiled, stood up and began to stretch his leg muscles. He beckoned Dixie to follow as he jogged away slowly on the return leg back to the barrack block. As they plodded along, Dixie admitted he really had underestimated his best pal. Their plan was really taking shape and Dixie was being swept along with Ben's enthusiasm to carry it out. He confessed to be very sceptical at first but the challenge and the buzz of achieving the impossible had firmly and definitely hooked Dixie. The fact that it could result in the loss of many lives was not an issue to him.... well not at that moment in time.

The next morning Ben was in work. He was walking past one of the numerous notice boards in the corridor outside of the crewroom, when he saw one of the junior pilots pinning up a freshly penned notice. Ben read the poster and a big beaming smile appeared on his face. It announced that the Wing Commander had offered three, back seat trips in a Tornado for the groundcrew. It was a way of thanking them for all the effort over the past 6 months. A draw would be made to pull out the three lucky names and Ben knew he just had to win one of those trips so he hurried off to the squadron admin room to register his name.

The draw was due to take place at the end of the week with the first flight scheduled before the end of the month, weather permitting of course. The remaining two flights would follow after the Taceval exercise. By the time the draw was closed for entries, there were eighteen names in the hat.

The Wing Commander drew the names out himself in the crewroom later that week. He pulled out the first name. It was Frankie Fuller, the squadron admin clerk. His name was greeted with hoots of good natured derision by the massed audience, him not being a technician of course. Frankie would have the first trip and he was almost patted into the ground by all the back-slapping he received. Ben was disappointed not to get the first place. But that was short lived because the Wing Commander then called out,

"Corporal Brownley wins the second trip."

It was met with a huge cheer of delight. Dixie shouted out from the back of the crowd,

" You jammy bastard, Benny Boy. Another day at work when you won't get your hands dirty." Ben looked over to Dixie and gave him a big thumbs up. Only they knew the significance of getting airborne for real in a Tornado. The third place went to one of the Armourers, who joked that he would only go up in a Tornado, if he fitted the ejection seat himself.

That evening Ben enjoyed several beers in the clubhouse, courtesy of Dixie. He had placed a small side bet with one of the other Fairies, that Ben would get one of the flights. Dixie chatted over a beer and pointed out to Ben that it was unfortunate that the flight would be too late to be of any use to their mission.

Ben replied:

" Well, we will have to do something about that won't we?"

" What do you mean, Ben?" Dixie said with a puzzled expression on his face.

Ben turned sideways in his seat to mask his now almost whispered conversation from any one else, who may have been listening,

" Just imagine if Frankie couldn't fly on the day...say, he had an accident, which prevented him from being fit to fly.

Then I would get his place wouldn't I?" Ben explained quietly to Dixie.

Dixie's face changed to one of horror as he comprehended Ben's sinister declaration of intent.

" You mean knobble him or harm him just so you can fly first. That's a bit over the top isn't it?" exclaimed Dixie, who was suddenly seeing a new and unpleasant side of his best pal.

"No, not hurt him" Ben hastily added, " Just prevent him from getting that first flight ...give him a dose of the runs or something like that. I'll work it out later on, but I need you to back me up, OK?"
Dixie nodded in silent, reluctant agreement and went for two more beers.

The next day in work, the three lucky airmen were given a brief on what they had to do in preparation for their flight. A medical examination was first on the agenda to ensure they were fit to go airborne in a fast jet. They then had to get fitted up for flying equipment. It was essential that the helmet was of the correct fit just in case they had to eject and they were also measured up for a flying suit and their details entered in a log book. This ensured, when they came to dress for the flight, the equipment could be easily identified and at hand. The final part of their preparation was carried out by one of the station PT Staff. Each of them had to hang in a parachute harness, which was secured to the gymnasium ceiling. This enabled them to practice the release drills from the harness. Finally a run through of how to board the one man dingy carried by the ejection seat completed the mandatory emergency drills. All three left the gym, bound for the squadron dispersal clutching tightly in their hands the much-prized 'Authority to Fly' chits.

The following Tuesday the station rugby team squad turned up for the first full training session of the season. It always started in August at Feldbruch and a large and enthusiastic crowd changed into their kit. The summer's over-indulgence of cold beer and barbecues was making its presence felt, as the fitness training taxed lazy muscles. The session was hard but essential, if the team wanted to reproduce the excellent results of the previous season. The Coach was happy with the efforts of the squad and promised them a short game of full contact rugby at the end of the session. This would help them to get back into thinking the game of rugby and they all relished the opportunity to play for real after the long summer sojourn.

Ten minutes after the kick off Ben was confronted with a situation that helped him to secure his Tornado flight later that week.

A passage of play had resulted in Frankie Fuller running at the defending forwards. A ruck had ensued. Ben was jogging towards the heap of bodies that indicated the presence of the ball and he saw an arm holding onto the ball, protruding out of the back of the mass of players. It was easily recognizable as that of Frankie Fuller. A tattoo of a rampant lion was unique amongst the much-tattooed rugby players of Feldbruch Panthers. Ben could hear and feel Dixie thundering up behind him. They bound together and hit the back of the ruck in an attempt to push the opposition off the ball. As they hit the immovable object in front off them, Ben dropped down onto his right knee. The snap from the bone of

Frankie's forearm could be heard all around the pitch, his screams of pain muffled by the heavy bodies of the combined packs, which engulfed him.

The Coach stopped play immediately. Unentwining the tangled bodies without inflicting more pain onto Frankie was not easy. He emerged from the bottom of the pile of players wincing in agony and holding his arm and his red swollen, deformed wrist was clear evidence that a trip to the local military hospital was called for. The rest of the training session was terminated prematurely. As the ambulance took Frankie away, the Coach called the squad together to ask how the injury had happened. Before Ben could say anything, Dixie confessed that it must have been his fault, explaining that he had slipped going into the ruck and had fallen onto the ball with his knee and probably Frank's arm as well. The Coach accepted the explanation and everyone agreed that injuries do happen during training. It was a simple fact of the game.

After Ben and Dixie had showered, they sat and sipped a well-earned beer together in the clubhouse. Ben turned to Dixie and said:

"Why did you take the blame for Frankie's injury? You know it was down to me!"

Dixie raised his beer to his lips and winked at Ben. After taking a long swig of his beer he replied:

" Don't be such a dipstick, Benny Boy. When it gets back to the squadron that Frankie can't go flying, because the next man in the queue has broken his arm. How did you think that will look?"

Ben was pleasantly shocked by his best mate's loyalty and added, as he clinked his glass against Dixie's,

"Front row forwards stick together - don't we?"

"Of course we do. So get the beers in, it's your round" replied Dixie in mock empathy.

At the end of that eventful week Ben went into work. However this time it was not to don his overalls but to dress in flying clothing in preparation for his first Tornado flight. In the briefing room he was paired up with Flight Lieutenant Randy Rapson who was acknowledged to be the best pilot on the squadron and a great favourite of the groundcrew. Rapson ran through the plan of the sortie. He explained that they would cross the North Sea shadowing another of the squadron's aircraft as it dropped practice bombs on one of the ranges along the east coast. After that they would stooge around over the sea and unusually, they had been given clearance to carry out a dummy attack on one of the redundant, unoccupied gas rigs in the North Sea. Then they would transit at high-level back to base. Flight Lieutenant Rapson ran through the emergency drills they would use in the unlikely event of having to eject. Ben hardly heard the final part of the brief as he was tingling with excitement at the thought of the bombing runs ahead. This was just what he needed, as it would give him the vital experience he craved to enable his next, self-flown, flight to be a success.

Ben walked out to the HAS with his pilot. They chatted about the flight, the weather and of all things, the latest test match score. Ben was too engrossed in thinking about the hour and a half ahead to register anything. He didn't even realize that Dixie had appeared. He'd come over and taken several photographs of Ben, in his flying kit climbing into the cockpit of the dual control training variant of the Tornado GR5. After being strapped in and the ejection seat safety pins had been removed, Ben's head finally came out of the clouds. He was sat on a live ejection seat and the engines were powering up ready for the off. Ben switched on 100% oxygen to clear his head as he listened to the pilot run through the pre-take off checks.

Finally the words from Rapson that called for the chocks to be removed sounded in Ben's headphones. A noticeable increase of engine revs prompted the aircraft to glide slowly forward. A test of the nose wheel steering after the aircraft had left the HAS entrance, resulted in the Tornado shimmying to the left then to the right then steering the nose of the aircraft straight down the dotted centre line of the taxyway. Dixie was stood on top of the squadron HQ building waving frantically at his mate, as the aircraft taxied past heading for the runway. Ben acknowledged Dixie's signal with a 'Top Gun' type salute as he peered through the dark visor of his helmet. Dixie responded with a two-fingered gesture back at Ben.

The aircraft only took a few minutes to reach the threshold of the main runway and was swiftly and skillfully lined up for take off after it had taxied slowly over the arrestor cable that stretched the width of the broad runway. Just as Ben had practiced in the simulator, the pilot accelerated both the engines up to 50 % afterburner and the brakes were released. The sudden surge of raw, untethered power was different from anything ever experienced by Ben. It nearly matched the rush of adrenaline that pulsed through Ben's body, as the Tornado raced forward. The aircraft roared down the runway and up into the air as the air speed indicator shot past 155 knots. It was so smooth Ben could hardly believe he was flying. As they reached the boundary of the airfield Flight Lieutenant Rapson spoke to Ben,

" Corporal Brownley, we're going vertical, OK?"

"Yes Sir." Ben responded in gleeful excitement.

Flight Lieutenant Rapson pulled back on the control stick and the aircraft's nose rose rapidly and pointed skywards at a blue patch of cloudless sky about ten thousand feet above. The manner in which the aircraft climbed up and beyond that hole almost took Ben's breath away. They finally levelled out at fifteen thousand feet to transit towards the east coast of England.

Ben scanned the blue sky above his cockpit. High above he saw a large three-engined airliner, which was probably a Tristar, cruising the air lane heading for UK airspace. Ben spotted movement in the mirrors mounted on the canopy. It was another Tornado formatting on them. It pulled alongside on the left hand wing and the navigator waved over to Ben. He noted that the other aircraft had a practice bomb carrier fitted underneath the fuselage and deduced that this must have been the aircraft they would shadow into the bombing range. Ben couldn't wait. There was a great deal of radio traffic on the channel that Ben was monitoring.   Their aircraft rapidly lost altitude as it approached the controlled airspace around the bombing range just north of Skegness. Ben had thought that they would have been alongside the attacking aircraft and he would see the small blue painted bombs leave the aircraft and hit the target. But that was not the case. Instead and for clear safety reasons they were about half a mile away and five hundred feet higher. All Ben saw was the aircraft dive towards the target; a small speck fell from under the fuselage and a puff of white smoke sprung up just in front of the large white canvas target. Ben was a little disappointed at what he saw but he did make a mental note of some very useful information of how to approach and execute the bombing run.

Ben's aircraft pulled up to the left, leaving the other aircraft to go into a second attack profile. Flight Lieutenant Rapsom explained that there was no benefit in shadowing the other aircraft a second time. Instead they were heading for Hemingsby to carry out a practice landing approach, which was only twenty miles from the range so it was only a matter of minutes before they were flying over the airfield and over Ben's old haunt. Peering out of the cockpit he saw the familiar sight of Bulk Aviation Fuel Installation - Number 6 below, as it flashed past. He had some unpleasant memories of that Fuel Installation and it immediately brought back the daunting image of Burton, in full flow bollicking mode, following Ben's last visit to that remote location of the airfield.

The aircraft suddenly rolled to the left as the pilot simultaneously applied the power of the two Rolls Royce engines, pointing the nose of the aircraft out towards the North Sea. Flight Lieutenant Rapson chatted to Ben over the intercom. He explained that they would fly over the redundant gas rig with a low pass then turn in on to a simulated bombing run. Ben spoke back to his pilot and asked if he wanted the navigation equipment and weapon systems turning on. As the aircraft was not armed, Rapson could not see any problem with Ben Brownley using the kit so he gave his consent. The Tornado flew towards the gas rig at five hundred above the sea the grey waves flashing by. They flew directly over the rig and, as Dixie had shown Ben back in the simulator, he pushed the button on the console, which automatically marked the exact co-ordinates of the gas rig. The wonders of the avionics computers, in an instant, calculated the exact attack profile to enable the imaginary bomb hit the target. The aircraft banked hard over to pull a tight 360-degree circle to put the rig directly ahead of the attacking Tornado. On the second run-in to the target with the navigation and weapon systems up and running, it would give the pilot the data he needed to successfully hit the simulated aiming point. As they turned onto the bombing run, the pilot talked through the way he would carry out the attack if it were for real. They levelled off at two hundred and fifty feet above the cold, choppy waves of the North Sea at the optimum speed of a steady four hundred knots. Ben was lapping up the wealth of information that Rapson was divulging. Finally as their aircraft flew directly over the oil rig, a tone sounded in the headset and it told the crew that the simulated bomb had been released. The pilot, naturally, claimed a direct hit.

Flight Lieutenant Rapson was pleased with his mock attack and spoke to Ben in the back cockpit,

"Nice work, Corporal Brownley. Ever thought of taking navigating up full time?"
Ben replied, as the aircraft climbed rapidly and headed eastwards towards Feldbruch,

"No sir, if I became aircrew, it'll be as a pilot for me or nothing. "
Rapson glanced into the mirrors in his cockpit and adjusted one slightly to see his rear seat passenger who was peering over the weapons systems display screens.

" So you fancy yourself as a jet jockey do you?" the pilot inquired.

"Yes, sir. " answered Ben eagerly.

"OK then, Corporal Brownley take hold of the stick in your cockpit and take us home. You have control. You have control." Flight Lieutenant Rapson stated correctly if somewhat melodramatically.

Ben took hold of his control column with his right hand and the throttles with his left. And with his feet resting on the rudders pedals, he could now steer the aircraft under the direction of the pilot. He had to keep within a certain height band and on a fairly accurate heading. It was a wonderful experience to actually be flying the aircraft himself. He had to admit that it was much like the simulator and it gave him a massive boost in confidence towards his planned, future, personal mission of revenge.

The airfield at Feldbruch was only twelve miles away and just visible in the distance at the height they were flying, when Randy Rapson called over the intercom to Ben,

" I have control. " as he prepared the aircraft to land back at their home base. The touchdown was very smooth and the thrust reverse motors screeched as four titanium buckets deployed to redirect forward the hot gaseous product of the two Rolls Royce engines, which rapidly brought the 30-ton aircraft to a slow taxiing speed. The pilot spoke again to his back seat occupant,

" Well Corporal. I hope you enjoyed that and I must say, I was impressed by your navigation but it appears you have rather a flair for flying the front seat. You should follow this up, you know... we'll talk about this back at the squadron."

The Tornado aircraft turned off the runway and headed back to the dispersal. It was marshalled into the front of the HAS and onto the chocks by Corporal Dixie Dean, who beamed a broad smile at his best mate.

CHAPTER 11

Ben Brownley felt like he was walking on air as he left the HAS following his flight in a Tornado as he made his way back at the flying clothing section to hand in his helmet and equipment. He hadn't noticed until he was back indoors, that his flying suit was soaking wet with perspiration. Ben quickly changed into dry clothes and went into the crewroom for a coffee and hopefully to tell Dixie all about his flight. Sat in the corner of the crewroom was Dixie he already had a steaming mug of coffee waiting for Ben. They chatted together for a while until Warrant Officer O'Reilly came and sat down opposite. O'Reilly spoke to Ben,

" Cpl Brownley, I trust you enjoyed your back seat trip?"

Ben replied that he had. However his beaming smile gave a reply that required no words. Warrant Officer O'Reilly was genuinely pleased for Ben and it was obvious that he had already spoken to Flight Lieutenant Rapson, because he then asked:

" I understand we have a budding pilot on our hands, or so young Rapson tells me...It must have been all that time you've been spending in the flight simulator."

Ben was absolutely dumbfounded at what O'Really O'Reilly had said. His eyes darted nervously towards Dixie, who had his mug up to his lips and was staring intensely into it hoping the crewroom floor would open up and swallow him.

Warrant Officer O'Reilly continued:

"I saw you two going into the simulator building the other evening. So, when I bumped into Chief Tech Cookson in the Sergeant's Mess last night, I asked him what you were up to."

Ben was feeling very uncomfortable by now and his pulse in his neck throbbed and suddenly doubled its cadence. O'Reilly smiled and admitted that he been surprised at what he had heard about his Corporal Brownley. Ben was now beginning to wriggle in his seat and Dixie kicked him under the table to calm him down. O'Really O'Reilly finally put them both out of their misery by saying:

" Well, I was surprised at first and that's a fact. But when Mick Cookson told me you were putting in a few extra hours in practicing your emergency engine drills, I must say, I was impressed. Well done, Brownley. Keep it up and we'll make a sergeant out of you yet." He rose from his seat; patted Ben on the shoulder and left the table.

Both Ben and Dixie were for once completely stumped for words. As Warrant Officer O'Reilly reached the door, he turned and spoke again:

"You know what Brownley? You should have asked Mick Cookson if you could have had a flight while you were in there. It would have made your back seat trip even better." Then the Warrant Officer disappeared out of sight down the corridor. Ben and Dixie said nothing for about ten seconds and then they both burst out laughing together.

The next day the first of the pre-Taceval exercise briefings were held. The Wing Commander stood up and spoke to the whole of the squadron, who had been mustered in one of the empty HASs and gave all squadron personnel a rousing pep talk and thanked aircrew and groundcrew alike for their superb effort so far. He also reminded everyone that one final big effort was essential to enable Taceval to be a success. The Sengo got up next and for once he did not spring any surprises on the groundcrew or the Jengo either. He also appeared to be in a remarkably good mood and was even complimentary towards the efforts of the groundcrew... for a change. But the sting in the tail was, that there was no sting in the tail! It left most of the young airmen feeling very suspicious. They had come to expect some new idea or policy change prior to every exercise but this time - nothing. Ben thought to himself that this was very unusual ... but there still was time before Taceval! It was only two weeks to go before that exercise. As they all dispersed following the briefing, there was some deep soul searching amongst the groundscrew, but it mattered little as everyone had to crack on with doing their job and hopefully keeping the Sengo in his unaccustomed good mood.

At the weekend Ben and Dixie went for their usual run together. They stopped, as had become the norm, at the glade for their mandatory rest break. As they sat on the grass they passed the time by throwing pine cones at a tree stump. Dixie had a direct hit and his cone ricocheted off into the bushes punching the air in delight at his marksmanship. He turned to Ben to ask how they would manage for money after they had gone AWOL in the Welsh mountains. Ben had already given this much consideration and had come up with a plan. He was brimming with confidence when he replied to Dixie:

" How much money have you got saved up in the bank?"

Dixie thought for a few moments and said:

" About a thousand quid, I suppose... but that won't last long when our wages get stopped"

" I know that," responded Ben, "I've got about two grand but we will need more, so this is the plan." Ben took a quick glance around the glade, leaned closer to his mate and continued in a hushed tone. "We both need to go into different German banks on Monday and get the biggest bank loan we can get. You can tell them you want to buy a Porche or something: you know they throw money at servicemen out here, so we won't have much problem." Dixie was listening carefully and concentrating hard on his buddy's master plan. Ben continued:

" The Friday before the exercise you'll need to go in and draw the money out in cash. You could tell them you've got a big discount for a cash sale. I'll do the same at my branch and we then go to each other's banks and exchange the Deutchmarks for Sterling or, at a push, for US Dollars. That should see us ok, for a while anyway. And, as we will not be coming back, the repayments won't matter anyway." Dixie was impressed with Ben's ingenuity and forward planning. They both jogged back to the barrack block at a leisurely pace, feeling content with the plan and its development so far.

Back in their accommodation block they were taking a shower in adjacent cubicles. As there was no one else in the ablutions, Dixie spoke:

"Benny Boy, we can't keep on referring our little visit to UK as the 'plan'. We should give it a code name, like they do to all military operations. What do you think? "

Ben chuckled, but agreed it would be most proper, so he asked Dixie, if he had any suggestions. Dixie stuck his head around the partition and into Ben's cubical. He smiled broadly and it was obvious he had already given it some thought. Dixie replied:

" How about Operation Empty Caddie?" Ben frowned and looked puzzelled at Dixie's idea. After a few seconds he responded:

" Go on then. Explain to me how you came up with that one?"

Dixie's inane grin broadened and he said:

" Well. When its ended there'll be no tea you see. Get it Benny Boy. No T-U-C.

Ben rubbed his hand over his soapy head and flicked a handful of suds in Dixie's direction, as a protest against his awful pun. Dixie retreated into his own cubical to resume showering. When they had finished, they were both drying themselves off, when Dixie spoke again,

" Seriously, Ben, I do have a suggestion. How about Operation Twickenham.... Because all rugby players, that's English ones of course, regard Twickenham as the Rugby Union's HQ and for that week in September, Llandudno pier will be TUC HQ. What do you think mate?"

Ben nodded his head slightly and replied:

" And of course the two of us talking about Twickers wouldn't raise an eyebrow around here amongst this crowd of Philistines and non-believers in God's chosen game."

Ben grinned and added after a few moments, "Yes, Dixie, Operation Twickenham is on!"

On Monday, while they ate their evening meal in the airman's mess, Ben was chatting quietly with Dixie. He asked whether, in the light of his back seat trip in the Tornado, if more simulator training was necessary or not. Dixie, for once, took the lead. He was adamant that they need to keep training on the simulator right up until the last possible moment. This would keep Mick Cookson on his toes. Dixie then explained that he also needed, at some time in the future, to run through the flight plan route of the mission on the simulator. Ben agreed and they both went to the simulator that evening.

Mick Cookson was not over-impressed; having to put in yet more hours of unofficial overtime to keep Brownley and Dean sweet. Reluctantly he powered up the rig in silence and let them both do their usual sortie. Once Ben and Dixie were strapped in and the engine running, they prepared for take-off but this time, as soon as they were airborne, Ben pulled back hard on the stick. The simulator rig tilted nose up a foot or so, which gave the sensation of the aircraft climbing steeply up. The altimeter indicated they were soon passing through the normal cruising height of fifteen thousand feet and they levelled out at twenty five thousand feet. Dixie's voice broke in over the intercom,

" That was different Benny Boy, What was that for?"
Ben wasn't sure whether Mick Cookson was listening into their conversation, so he replied:
" Just for the hell of it!"

Flying at that height meant that Dixie had to alter the scale of the moving map that both cockpits displayed. Ben carefully studied the map image displayed on the screen before him. When the UK coast finally appeared at the top of the screen, their heading had resulted in them approaching the coast just south of Cleethorpes. Ben pushed the stick forward and rapidly dived down to within a few hundred feet of the sea. Dixie piped up again,

"And I suppose that was for the hell of it as well?"

" Affirmative " came Ben's' reply.

They flew for a while following the route fed into the navigation computer by Dixie. Ben was getting a little bored with just flying around. After a while he spoke into his microphone, asking Mick Cookson to throw in a few faults or system failures to give him something different or novel to do. There was no response from Mick. In Cookson's absence Dixie took the opportunity, during the transit back to base, to tell Ben how he intended to achieve his part of operation Twickenham.

Dixie explained that, unlike the simulated bombing run that Ben had tried out against the gas rig during his real flight and where his aircraft had to over-fly the target to get a 'fix' for the computer, but he had devised an alternative plan. Ben was eager to hear and was pleased that his back seat partner was playing a full role in the mission. Dixie elaborated further,

" As soon as I get the chance. I'll go into the aircrew mission planing cell and create our mission, which I'll record onto the usual cassette tape. I'll be able to then load it into the aircraft's navigation and weapon system, before we take off. We'll retain the element of surprise during the attack and get away quicker just in case there are other aircraft in the area. All I need is the co-ordinates of the target and of any points we need to over-fly on route. Have you got any places you want to use as waypoints?"

Ben thought hard for a few moments. Despite the fact that he had not considered that any other aircraft would be in the area, he replied,

" Yes, Hemingsby; the steel works were Wally used to work; the target of course and then finish off with Capel Curig, which is where we'll bang out. Will that do?"
Jokingly, Dixie confirmed the instructions with,

"OK skipper, rogered and out!"
Ben turned his attention to his preparation for landing. He called for Dixie to lend a hand to talk him down onto the runway. As had happened on previous landings, Ben was looking good until the final few hundred feet and then he lost control of the direction of the aircraft and ended up trying to land on the grass to the left of the runway. A white screen and juddering cockpit signalled yet another unsuccessful landing for Ben. They both climbed out of the cockpit and as they left the rig room, they saw Mick Cookson sprawled out over the console apparently fast asleep. Ben didn't bother to wake him but he pulled the master switch, which powered down the rig room, before Dixie and he left the building.

Early the following morning aided by Ben, Dixie slid quietly into the mission planning cell on the squadron dispersal; it was well before any aircrew where around. Using the computerized navigation plotting table, crews were able to pin-point the target and each of the waypoint co-ordinates. They utilized a device not unlike a computer mouse, which was integrated with a magnifying glass and the two faint black lines crossing at right angles to each other were placed directly over the feature or co-ordinate on the mapping table and, with a click of the button, it would record the data. This data was then converted into a code, transferred onto a tape, so that the aircraft's navigation system could be uploaded. The aircraft's computer systems could decipher the code and guide the aircraft to those points with precise and faultless accuracy.

That evening Ben and Dixie couldn't wait to try out the mission tape they'd put together that morning. Turning up at their usual time at the simulator building, they knocked on the door and waited for Mick Cookson to open up. Instead a corporal, whom they didn't recognize, unlocked and opened the door. He told them both that, Chief Technician Cookson had been sent home on sick leave by the Medical Officer. He explained that Chiefy Cookson had been found slumped over the console by the RAF Police during their security check the previous evening. The corporal, drunk with the power of being left in charge of the simulator building, would not allow Ben or Dixie into the building and with a hint of arrogance he quickly closed and locked the door leaving them standing outside. Ben and Dixie were a little shocked by the news of Mick Cookson. Despite the fact that they had been using him for their own ends, they didn't wish him any harm.

As they ambled slowly back to the barrack block, Ben admitted to Dixie that the option to try out their route on the simulator was now out of the question. Their only alternative would be to try it and test it during their mission. Dixie was not overjoyed with that prospect but, as in character to the situation, he calmly shrugged his shoulders in reluctant acceptance of its inevitability.

Back in work the following day, Ben was met by the prospects of a considerable workload. The Sengo in his infinite wisdom had decided that at least two of the Tornadoes required an engine to be replaced before the up and coming exercise. They were down a little on max power thrust and in normal circumstances low thrust would be closely monitored by the propulsion tradesmen and the engine would only be changed, when it was at the bottom of the set limits for thrust. However Taceval was very important to the squadron, so the Sengo wouldn't take the risk of any of them failing during the exercise. The extra work would ensure Ben would be kept extremely busy and his chances of getting time off to play the first game of the season that very afternoon were slim to none.

Ben plucked up the courage to ask Jengo Simpson, if he could play. After consulting with Warrant Officer O'Reilly, he gave his consent. However it was on the condition that after the game, Ben would go back to the squadron to help the night shift to finish the work. Ben was so keen to play, he accepted the Jengo's caveat and probably would have accepted any condition at that particular moment in time.

The game was against RAF Hemingsby; Ben's previous teammates who were on a pre-season tour in Germany. It was a very physical but clean match. After a nervous start by both teams it soon blossomed into quite an exhibition for the rugby purists. Therefore the ten points apiece draw was a fair result for a well-fought game.

Showered and dressed back in his uniform, Ben had a quick drink of shandy and he left Dixie at the bar, while he cycled back to the squadron dispersal.

By 9:30 pm, Ben had finished and had been stood down from work. He went back to the clubhouse for a quick beer, before the barman finally called last orders. The bar was packed and smoke filled. Most of the players were still there; many of them had been joined by their wives or girlfriends. Dixie was extremely inebriated again and he was being ably supported under the armpits by two young ladies, as he re-told his story of how he scored his spectacular try during the game. In reality, he fell over the try line clutching the ball whilst being propelled by all of the Feldbruch's forwards.... but Dixie loved to flower it up somewhat.

Ben suddenly caught a glimps of a familiar face in the corner of the bar. It was Mick Cookson and he was alone and drinking heavily. Ben went over and sat next to him. Through his bleary eyes Cookson recognized Ben and in a drunken slur he spoke,

" What d'you want? If it's about your Warrant Officer, I only told him that you were being good little engineers, so you needn't worry."
Ben told Cookson that he already knew, but he asked,

" I understand you've been unwell."
Mick Cookson cradled his head in his hands and replied sharply:

" What do you care anyway.... you're only interested in me for the simulator, just piss off and leave me alone."

"You're wrong Mick" replied Ben, "Anyway we won't be coming anymore so you can forget about it now."

He then added " And our little secret is also forgotten and it won't be mentioned ever again."

Mick Cookson stared at Ben. He did not change his expression or respond to Ben's statement instead he stood up, left the table and headed, unsteadily on his feet, towards the toilets.

Ben remained sat where he was. He looked towards the bar, and saw Dixie who by now, was trying to walk the length of the bar, while balancing a full pint of ale on his head. Suddenly two young ladies came and sat either side of Ben. One of them was Samantha Burton. She was giggling and it was obvious she was more than a little tipsy. Ben walked over to her and told her quietly that she should go home, as she would only get the club into trouble by drinking under age. But she just fluttered her eyes at Ben and ignored his protests. Ben sniffed at the drink she had in her hand; it was orange juice stinking of aniseed and easily recognizable as a Harvey Wallbanger and a potent brew for any young girl, Ben thought to himself.

He tried again to persuade her to leave the bar but she wouldn't move. Ben put his hands on each of her arms to try and ease her to her feet and hopefully out of the bar. Just at that moment Mick Cookson reappeared from the toilet and was met with Ben with his hands around young Samantha. Cookson glared at them both and as he turned to walk away he said,

"So the blackmailer and his slag are finally together!"

Ben tried to stand up and follow him, but Samantha clung to him giggling like the schoolgirl she was. Cookson staggered more than he walked, bumping into several people, as he exited the clubhouse door. But Ben was firmly held captive by the two young girls and as he didn't want to make a scene, which would have damaged his 'street-cred', he stood and endured his young female restraint. Some of the team muttered the occasional comment on Ben's envious predicament as he was framed be the two pretty females. However the rest of the lads didn't know how old Samantha really was. Ben tolerated the situation as long as he could. But, as he started to make a move to extradite himself, Samantha looked longingly into his eyes and said:

" Cpl Brownley, I never thanked you for saving me from that horrible, perverted Cookson chap " and she threw her arms around Ben, kissed him passionately on his lips and wouldn't let him go until she had her fill of his inviting lips. Ben tried to repel her amorous advances without loosing face with his mates, who were soon loudly applauding the loving embrace they were all witnessing. Ben decided not to fight it. He relented, closed his eyes and let her continue and hoped she would finally let him go. But he gradually became aware that the cheering and jibes of his team mates had stopped. He opened his eyes to see the reason why.

" Oh shit"! Ben mumbled in disbelief through his compressed lips. He saw, who was standing in front of his table. It was Samantha's father...Squadron Leader Julian Burton. The look on Burton's face was one of pure anger. He spoke to his daughter through his tightly clenched teeth so as to limit the volume of his voice.

" You're coming home now young lady!" He gripped Samantha by the arm and pulled her roughly from the seat. Then, leaning over to get close to Ben's ear, and in a menacing tone he said,

143

'   " I'll see you tomorrow Brownley. This time you've gone too far and by God, you'll pay for this." Burton then frog marched his daughter out of the bar leaving Ben to contemplate the latest of his faux pas. Everyone in the clubhouse bar was stunned into absolute silence - but it was very short-lived and without any signal, they all started chatting together and carried on as if nothing had happened. Ben pushed away his half-full glass of beer and trudged forlornly out of the clubhouse back to his barrack block. He only hoped that whatever Burton had lined up as retribution for kissing his young daughter, it wouldn't impact on what he and Dixie had been working so hard at over the past several months.

CHAPTER 12

Cycling slowly up the path, which led to the squadron groundcrew accommodation building, Ben braked in front of the main entrance and dismounted from his bicycle. Inside the building he headed for the locker room, removing his rucksack as he walked. Flight Lieutenant Simpson shouted him from the other end of the corridor,

" Cpl Brownley. My office, when you've changed, I need to speak to you urgently."

Ben knew what was about to come so he replied rather reluctantly,

" Yes, Sir."

Jengo Simpson replied sharply and somewhat impatiently,

" And look lively about it, I haven't got all day."

Ben changed quickly into his overalls and hurried down to Simpson's office. He didn't know why he was in such a hurry to receive what, he just knew, amounted to bad news. He knocked on the half-open door. Flight Lieutenant Simpson invited him in and in a very serious tone of voice he spoke to Ben,

" Cpl Brownley the Sengo has told me all about last night and how he discovered his young daughter in the rugby club with you." He waited a few seconds and continued, " It appears you seem to have a death wish, when it comes to the Sengo. He's really got it in for you after this latest stunt and I don't think I'll be able to help you this time."

Ben interrupted his Jengo and tried to explain why he was caught kissing young Samantha and waffled on about her being drunk and how she just grabbed him and kissed him. Flt Lt Simpson listened to Brownley. At the end of Ben's earnest plea in his own defence Jengo Simpson admitted that he was actually a little sympathetic towards his young corporal's dilemma, but before he could respond any further, the telephone rang. He answered it, listening carefully but saying very little in reply. After he'd put the receiver down he turned to Ben and told him to come back to see him later, as he had an important matter to deal with. Ben made a half-hearted attempt to stand to attention before he turned and left the office.

Later on that day, Jengo Simpson popped his head inside the crewroom door and beckoned Ben over to him.

"We need to continue our talk, Cpl Brownley... follow me." said Simpson and he ushered Ben towards his office door. Even before Ben was sat down Flight Lieutenant Simpson started to speak,

" Well Cpl Brownley it looks as if you've managed to escape the wrath of the Sengo again....for a while at least." Simpson continued:

" The Sengo still wants you to account for your actions with his daughter last night but that will have to wait until after the exercise. That phone call I had, while you were in my office, was about Sergeant Asquith, your shift boss. He's been sent on compassionate leave because his wife has given birth prematurely. That, of course, makes you the senior propulsion tradesman on your shift and you'll have to run the engine team throughout Taceval."

Ben half smiled at the thought of being in charge of the shift. Confidently he told the Jengo that he would not let him down. Jengo Simpson acknowledged Ben's bold statement and added:

" You will not be letting me down if you screw up Cpl Brownley, but you'll be letting yourself down. And don't forget, if you do manage to do a half decent job of it, then maybe and only maybe, Sengo might be a little lenient with you." Ben nodded and stood up to leave the office, his heart feeling a great deal lighter. As he reached the door he turned and spoke to Jengo Simpson,

" Sir. There is one thing. How did the Sengo know that Samantha, sorry Miss Burton, was in the rugby club with me?"

Flight Lieutenant Simpson was searching through his in-tray. He looked up and answered the question,

" Oh, Yes. The Sengo told me that he was out looking for his daughter, who was far later coming home than she should have been. Apparently he bumped into that chief who runs the flight simulator. I understand that the chief had been drinking...I just can't remember his name at the moment"

Ben interrupted:

" You mean Chief Tech Cookson? "

Jengo Simpson nodded in agreement and replied: " Yes, that's the guy. Sengo asked him, if he'd seen a young girl with long blonde hair. Chiefy Cookson had said that sounded like the girl drinking in the rugby club with Cpl Brownley, And of course the rest you know."

Ben left the office. He didn't blame Mick Cookson for dropping him in it with the Sengo and it could have been much worse.   Most   important   was   the   fact   that   any punishment that Burton had already dreamt up had been put on hold until after the exercise. An exercise, of course in which Corporal Ben Brownley would not actually be partaking.

The rest of the week went by extremely swiftly with Ben busy running the engine trade on his shift. There was the usual host of pre-exercise jobs that needed completing and he was really beginning to enjoy the new responsibilities that had been thrust upon him. Ben managed to keep out of the Sengo's way, who was also very busy. For once he'd left the running of the shift to the Jengo, which was received with much delight by of all of the groundcrew and by Friday everything was in the advance stages of preparation for the imminent and very important exercise. Ben and Dixie managed to use their lunch break to drive down to their respective banks and draw out the large cash loan they'd both arranged. They changed it into Sterling and were back onto the squadron dispersal, before anyone had realised they'd been away.

Before the shift ended, Warrant Officer O'Reilly summoned everyone into the crewroom for a pre-exercise brief. As had been anticipated weeks before by both Ben and Dixie, the Warrant Officer explained that the following Monday would be a normal working day and confirmed that the final preparation and the arming of the aircraft would be carried out on that day. And on the Tuesday, it being a German public holiday, the squadron and the station would be stood down and he concluded the brief by adding a word of caution, which generally was received more as a directive than a suggestion, that it would enable everyone to get a good rest before the exercise.

Ben looked over towards Dixie, who was stood by the window and he exchanged a knowing wink of an eye with his best mate as they both began to realise just how Operation Twickenham would effect the exercise let alone both their futures. They were extremely pleased to know that it would really screw things up but best of all it was the thought that Sengo would, at the very least, probably burst a major blood vessel.

WO O'Reilly finished off the brief with a plea for two volunteers to man the dispersal on the Tuesday. Ben looked over towards Dixie, who moved to raise his arm. Ben shook his head and furrowed his brow in an attempt to telegraph to his mate that he needed to wait a moment and he didn't want to appear too keen to volunteer for the onerous task of guard duty during a station stand-down. The Warrant Officer didn't get any takers so Ben waited about twenty seconds or so, then he nodded to Dixie and they both raised their hands together.

After the briefing was concluded and the crew room slowly emptied of the groundcrew, Warrant Officer came over to Ben and Dixie. He thanked them for offering their help and told them to come and see him for a briefing on Monday, adding jokingly that he didn't expect a repeat of what happened last time his pair of wayward corporals had baby-sat the squadron's dispersal prior to an exercise. Dixie responded cheekily by boldly announcing,

" Do not worry Sir, you can be confident that the outcome of us guarding the dispersal will be totally different from what happened last time."

" Oh really is that a fact. I'm so glad to hear it" replied Warrant Officer O'Reilly. Both Ben and Dixie smiled knowingly at the predictable retort from the WO.

That evening Ben was late leaving the squadron dispersal, as he had to do the final check out of all the tool kits prior to the exercise. During his cycle ride back to his barrack block, Ben was still recalling with some amusement Dixie's audacious comments to O'Reilly.

He didn't see Dixie until just after seven o'clock, when he turned up at Ben's room. Dixie was clutching his rucksack, as if it contained the crown jewels. Once inside the room he opened up the bag to reveal fifteen thousand pounds in crisp, clean notes. Ben chuckled, opened his locker and rummaging around he extracted a plastic NAAFI carrier bag, which contained a similar amount bundled into thousand pound packages. Dixie had never seen so much money before and in a slightly croaky voice he asked Ben,

"What am I going to do with this lot? It won't fit into my wallet."

Ben was mildly amused at Dixie's predicament; one for which as always he had already calculated. This time he reached into his other locker and pulled out two money belts. Dangling them in front of Dixie, he explained:

" There's one for you and one for me. They'll hold all the notes you've got there and on Tuesday you can wear it under your flying suit."

"Brilliant! Is there anything that you haven't thought about." Dixie said with genuine admiration for Ben's forethought. Ben sat back on his bed and raised his eyes to the ceiling and after a few moments had elapsed, he responded to Dixie's compliment. With a trace of a lump in his throat and a tear glistening in the corner of his eyes he spoke softly to Dixie,

"The whole operation to gain revenge for Wally's death has haunted me ever since his funeral. Every night before I went off to sleep or even if I had a just moment spare to myself, I thought and planned about nothing else. My ultimate ambition is to destroy those bastards who orchestrated the strike, which as far as I'm concerned killed Wally. I've dissected every scenario I could think of to come up with several options for each possible situation. Yes Dixie I think I have thought about every eventuality and Operation Twickenham will run like a well oiled machine."

Dixie listened to Ben, as he was stuffing the bank notes into his own money belt. He had the utmost confidence in his mate and was evidently overtaken by the enthusiasm and passion emitted by Ben. They were both fired up to obliterate the union hierarchy and their intended target would be congregating at the TUC annual conference within a few days.

On Saturday evening Ben and Dixie tried hard not to give the impression that it was to be their last weekend in Germany but it was very difficult not to do so. A party was underway in the clubhouse and an obscene amount of free beer had been provided by the hosts. They didn't know who that was but it didn't matter anyway as they both circulated amongst their friends and team-mates to say a clandestine farewell; not that any of the recipients were sober enough to realise it was a farewell.

It had started to give Ben and Dixie quite a buzz to know that they alone were privy to the details of Operation

Twickenham. They were both in extremely high spirits and just after midnight they slid away back to their barrack block. It was time, for once, to go steady on the beer and Ben was certain that they didn't want to risk loosing control of their tongues. Temperance was therefore the best policy, and was a definite first for both of them. Being so close to their final goal, they could not fall at this late stage.

When Sunday morning dawned, it was drizzling with rain. Ben decided that he would pass on his usual run so he turned over and went back to sleep. Half an hour later Dixie was banging on the room door. He wasn't going to let a little rain stop him from going for a run and was wearing his running kit under his a waterproof jogging suit. Reluctantly Ben dressed and they set off along their usual route, dodging and hopping over the puddles as they ran.

By the time they'd reached their usual stopping place it was pouring with rain and there was the threat of thunder and lightning in the air. Despite being told to never shelter under a tree, when there is lightning about; they had no choice. With their backs to the gnarled trunk of a very large tree, they sat in silence for several minutes.

Ben finally broke the peace and tranquillity of the pleasant, wooded spot, which they had began to regard as their own. He turned to Dixie and spoke:

" I know that my urge to avenge Wally's death has sucked you into this crazy plan. But this is my fight, so if you want to pull out now before it's too late, I'll understand. After all it's not your problem and you've a lot more to loose." Ben then turned his head away. A small tear had formed in his eye. He found it hard to face his best mate after offering him an escape route and the emotion of what they were about to set out to do finally seemed to be getting to Ben. Dixie sensed the emotional predicament Ben was in and responded in his usual unabashed manner,

" Not bloody likely! And if you think that you can go swanning off to UK for some fun and games without me, then you're sadly mistaken, Benny Boy. Anyway, you couldn't manage without me, could you?" Dixie held out his hand to Ben. They shook on Operation Twickenham - vowing to see it through... together.

An early start was scheduled for the whole of B Shift on 701 Squadron the following Monday morning. It was still raining and it suddenly occurred to Ben that the weather was the only thing that he hadn't calculated for. Bad weather would be a real problem for him. To fly the aircraft would be hard enough but to do it in bad weather and poor visibility that was something completely different, so as soon as the Met Office was manned, he rang up to check the forecast. Ben felt a little more comfortable, when he learned that the rain would only persist throughout the rest of the day. The good news was that scattered showers and sunny periods would prevail over all of Western Europe and UK for the next few days. Ben crossed his fingers and prayed that the weather would not result in the months of their planning to go to waste. He realised that there would definitely be no second chance to complete Operation Twickenham.

It was a very busy day with the preparation of the aircraft in readiness for the exercise. Convoys of vehicles towed the thousand pound bombs from the weapon storage areas and snaked their way into and around the dispersal;

depositing their menacing load outside the entrance of every HAS in turn. Each aircraft would be loaded with two of those green menacing high explosive bombs. As soon as they were securely tethered to the bomb release ejector units of the aircraft, the strict weapon and explosive safety rules came into force. As Sengo toured the HAS's, checking everything was running on time, Ben was driving a tractor towing a generator into one of the HASs, when he came face to face with the Sengo. Ben thought he'd better take the initiative and cheerily offered Squadron Leader Burton a 'good morning Sir. ' greeting. Burton nodded but did not reply at first. A few moments later he walked up close to Ben, who was uncoupling a trailer from the back of the tractor. The Sengo spoke,

"Cpl Brownley, I understand you and Cpl Dean have volunteered to guard the dispersal again prior to the exercise."

" Yes Sir, We thought that after we let you down last time, it was only right that we should volunteer again and do it correctly this time." responded Ben trying hard not to appear over-patronizing.

" A most admirable offer, Cpl Brownley. However my confidence in you is far less then you have in yourself. I accept that you'll be guarding the dispersal and my aircraft but to give me peace of mind you will be accompanied by Sergeant Goodwin, the squadron admin SNCO. He will stay on the dispersal carrying on doing his own work but also keeping an eye on you at the same time. I shouldn't have to do this but this exercise is far too important for the squadron to leave anything to chance." Burton walked away leaving Ben nonplused at the prospect of having the Sengo's spy in their midst, while they tried to pull off Operation Twickenham. Ben drove off to find Dixie as they needed to talk about what they were going to do with Sgt Goodwin.

Dixie was down by the rubbish skips. He was emptying the bins from the crewroom, when Ben finally caught up with him. Ben checked that there was no one else around and he told Dixie what Sengo had said. Dixie did not appear to be phased at all about the introduction of Sgt Goodwin on the day they'd planned to steal a twenty million pound aircraft. He just carried on emptying the bins, which succeeded in getting Ben a little agitated at his lack of interest or concern. Dixie stopped and spoke to Ben,

" Don't worry Benny Boy, we'll think of something. I'm sure that the massive bulk of Sergeant Aubery Goodwin, all nine stone soaking wet of him, won't cause us too many problems. We'll bag and tag him and bung him the paperwork storage cupboard if necessary." Ben saw a new, more ruthless side of Dixie. However, when put into context of tying up someone and roughing them up or bombing a whole auditorium of people, it really wasn't all that bad.

They both walked back to the groundcrew accommodation building, as it was time to receive their guarding brief from Warrant Officer O'Reilly. It was very similar to the last briefing they had received from O'Really O'Reilly but with much more emphasis on the timely refueling of the tractor this time. He restated his cautious word of warning, which meant that they must not do anything that would give the Sengo any reason to find fault in their actions either before, during or after the exercise. Ben had grown to admire his Warrant Officer. He wasn't a bad old stick and he had extracted them out of the mire on the odd occasion but Ben did have a twinge of guilt that, after they've misappropriated the Tornado aircraft, no blame could be attributed to either the Warrant or the Jengo. Ben could only hope that when the brown stuff hit the fan, and as sure that night follows day that it would, the whole pile of it would land exclusively on top of Squadron Leader Julian Burton.

Warrant Officer O'Reilly smiled at his two reprobate corporals as he concluded the briefing by telling them that, following a successful outcome of the exercise, the squadron would be stood down for a weeks leave. He told them that personally he would be going back to Ireland to see his grandchildren. He asked Ben and Dixie where they would be spending their hard-earned leave. Dixie replied first and a wicked glint erupted in his eyes:

" I'm off to Twickenham, Sir."

Ben could hardly contain his mirth at Dixie's outrageous but truthful answer. He replied with his own stab at secretive humour,

" And I'm off to Snowdonia, Sir."

Dixie chuckled at the surreptitious repartee that they had both spontaneously generated. Ben and Dixie left the office to change out of their uniforms and go back to the airman's mess for their evening meal.

The guarding of the squadron dispersal that evening would be carried out by some of the night shift personnel, who would remain over-night. Ben and Dixie were detailed to take the handover of the dispersal at 0600 hours, Tuesday. Sergeant Goodwin would, under the instruction of the Sengo, pitch up at 0800 hours.

That evening many of the single airmen went to the rugby clubhouse for a beer. Even though it would be their last chance to have a drink for a few days, most did take it easy and only had a couple of beers. Both Ben and Dixie had pledged to each other to have a quiet night and it was the hardest thing they had ever done. Dixie was even heard to turn down a beer and the last time that happened it nearly made the national newspapers. But true to their vow they kept their alcoholic intake to a couple of Warstieners and they left the clubhouse to get their heads down, before the early start of what was scheduled to be, a momentous day.

CHAPTER 13

Well before his alarm clock burst into life announcing that it was 0445, Ben had lay awake in his bed listening to the dawn chorus of chattering wild birds, who were perched in the trees outside his window. The early morning sunshine stabbed through the gap in the curtains like a laser and its presence told him that the rain had abated and the weather was unlikely to raise any cause of concern for Operation Twickenham. He knew, whatever the outcome of that day, it would undoubtedly be the most significant of his short and relatively uneventful life. He threw back the duvet and shuffled along the corridor in his flip-flops for a quick shower, before going for breakfast in the airmen's mess. He met Dixie at the breakfast bar in the mess as arranged. They both believed that a substantial meal was essential before what they had planned.... it could be a their last decent meal for some time. Consuming the huge fry-up was carried out in comparative silence; their innermost thoughts were both attuned to the same subject.

Suitably fed and watered, Ben and Dixie returned to their respective rooms. Ben dressed ready for the cycle ride into work and, as he reached for the door handle, he realized that it would be the last time he'd stand in his little home from home. He looked around the room to see if there was anything that he could take with him as a memento. Having only had a small rucksack, which was already occupied by his well-endowed money belt, it limited his choice. Also, as he needed to eject out of the aircraft later that day, it restricted his choice even further. Ben glanced at his autographed photograph of his rugby hero, Gareth Edwards, which was hanging over his bed but he decided that he couldn't even take that without the risk of damaging it.... and that would be sacrilege. Ben opted for the molten remains of Wally's Swiss army penknife, which was laid on the top of his bedside locker. He pushed it into his pocket and closed and locked the room door behind him.

Dixie was already in work when Ben arrived just before six a.m. He had already taken the handover from the night shift guards, who'd reported that they'd had a very quiet, uneventful night. As soon as the night shift had left the dispersal, Ben and Dixie set Operation Twickenham underway.

The first thing Ben and Dixie needed was to go into the engineering control room to decide their plan for the day and to select which aircraft they would use. Looking up at the aircraft state board, which was attached to the wall, it was pleasing, if not unexpected, to see that all of the squadron's aircraft were serviceable, armed and available.

Every Tornado squadron had a unique identification letter, which was painted on the tail of its aircraft. 701 Squadron's ident letter was A for Alpha. The first tail-letter was followed by another letter for each of the aircraft. Dixie scanned the list of the twelve aircraft, looking at each of the tail letters in turn. He wanted to go for Alpha Delta, as they were his real initials but Ben being more practical, opted for Alpha Lima. He knew that it had the best engines and the radar system was often reported by the aircrew to be the most reliable on the squadron. Alpha Lima needed to be prepared for flight and there were several other tasks that needed sorting, before Sergeant Goodwin arrived.

Dixie unlocked the small HAS access door where Alpha Lima was housed and, joined by Ben, they both stepped into its echoing vaults. Every footstep reverberated around the walls of its tomb-like, concrete enclosure. It was no different from any other time that they had entered a HAS early in the morning: this time, however, it seemed so much more ominous. Alpha Lima looked mean, menacing and every inch a war machine in its slate grey livery. Two 1000-pound bombs, which were painted olive green with a yellow band round the nose, nestled cozily beneath the fuselage. The presence of the arming safety pins were betrayed by the vivid red warning flags that hung limp in the still air of the HAS. It only took twenty-five minutes for both of them to prepare the aircraft for flight, which included the fitting of the essential liquid oxygen pot that would sustain their life, when the aircraft ventured into the thin air of the stratosphere.

Ben checked the electrical generator set, double-checked that all the ground equipment in the HAS had been moved outside to give the maximum room for the aircraft to taxy out. The two huge steel front doors of the HAS were opened to reveal a cavernous entrance, the sunlight beamed in caressing and warming the cold grey painted fuselage. The smaller rear doors, which allowed the engine exhaust fumes to exit the HAS, were slid apart. Those gapping apertures permitted the escape of the numerous sound waves and silenced the echoing tones generated from within the HAS.

Normally a tradesman would be positioned on each side of the doorway to guide the pilot as the aircraft taxied through the front doorway, as there was only a few feet each side of the aircraft's wing tip to spare. Next time Alpha Lima would be travelling through these doors there would be no assistance available. Ben had the daunting task of steering the aircraft out of the front doors; then the doors would seem very narrow indeed.

There was over an hour left before Sergeant Goodwin was due to arrive. Ben wanted to go into the flying clothing section to sort out their kit but Dixie had another task in mind. He told Ben to follow him into the Flight Planning room. First, Ben had to visit the toilet, as his nerves were affecting his bladder. He walked into the nearby toilet and stood at the urinal casually reading the graffiti that had been added to a poster, which was stuck to the wall. It read: ' If flying was difficult - then the groundcrew would have to do it!' Ben smiled at the well used and, in this case, ironic statement. He smiled to himself and silently wished that he had a pound for every time he'd seen it adoring a toilet wall.

Ben turned up at the flight planning facility a few minutes later. Dixie had already set up the plotting table and he had already loaded the mission tape into the computer, which he had produced previously. Dixie explained he had to finalize their mission route and he needed Ben's help.

Ben responded confidently that the first leg would be from Feldbruch and then onto Hemingsby; that route would have to be 'as required' because if they were to be shadowing an airliner, it would not be necessary to plan a specific route. Dixie confirmed to Ben that he would be able to provide directions to RAF Hemingsby as soon as they flew into UK airspace. He then ran through the route he had pre-programmed,

"From Hemingsby and on to the next way-point at Brymbo Steelworks would be almost in a straight line due west. We then turn onto a heading of 320 degrees towards the North Wales coast, crossing it at Abergele. For the final run-in to the target we will run parallel to the coast and after hitting and over-flying the target, we'll turn sharp onto a south-west heading for a few miles then turning due south, we continue until we over-fly Capel Curig." That was as far as Dixie had planned and programmed it into the computer. He needed to establish the rest of the escape details.

To help Ben in this matter, Dixie then suggested:

" I think we need to fly over Capel Curig and turn the aircraft onto a heading of 270 degrees. Between the two large wooded areas, just north of Dolwyddellan, I propose we eject about here." Dixie pointed to the map and at approximately 2 miles south of the village of Capel Curig, which showed a relatively flat area between two large forests that would be easily recognizable from the air. Dixie continued:

"If we leave the aircraft around that point at ...say two thousand feet, the aircraft, minus both of us of course, will fly on towards Snowdon. It should hit the mountains at least five or six miles away in an uninhabited area of rocky terrain."

Ben interjected:

" Brilliant, Dixie, that means we can use the forested area to the west for cover until it's dark and then we can walk down to Uncle Percy's farm."

"That's right, Benny Boy, but I do need to know exactly were the farm is ...just in case we get split up" enquired Diixie.

Ben traced along the map with his index finger. He followed the A4086 about a mile and a half west of Capel

Curig and circled two isolated buildings on the map with his fingertip, where the buildings were located on the hillside.

"There it is Dixie, there's the Hendre, just off the road on the 200 metre contour line and higher up at 300 meter line is the Hafod. And there you can see the footpath from the wooded area, where we will be holed-up in." Ben exclaimed with confidence.

They both were happy with the route and the escape plan they had devised. Before they left the room, Dixie took an ordinance survey map from the map cupboard. He drew a rough circle around the area with a luminous marker pen, where they would be ejecting and also the location both of Uncle Percy's farmhouses. He told Ben this was the back-up, if it all went to cock. Folding the map up carefully, Dixie pushed it into his back pocket.

Feeling very pleased with their plan, they both ran down the corridor towards the flying clothing section. It was just approaching 0710 hours and Sergeant Goodwin was due to arrive in fifty minutes time. Locating the flying kit for Ben was straight forward as he would be using the same equipment that he had worn when he went airborne last time. Dixie proved to be more problematic. His muscular frame was not easy to match with flying clothing used by the 701 Squadron aircrew, but Dixie finally found a flying suit he could squeeze into. They both decided not to use anti-g suits but they did each pick out a flying jacket to wear. The green, warm and waterproof jackets may prove to be very useful following their ejection as they weren't certain what weather the Welsh hillside may have in store for them.

When Ben went flying previously, the safety equipment fitter went to great pains to ensure the flying helmet was a precise fit. Dixie didn't have that luxury. So he went through the whole line of helmets that were carefully stowed in a large, pigeon-holed rack mounted against one of the walls. Finally, he found one that felt a bit wobbly...but would do. They both stood fully dressed ready to fly and were admiring themselves in a mirror with some mild amusement. The two Corporals were fooling around with their dark sun visors down and their oxygen facemasks fitted and were mimicking the aircrew-talk, when the door opened.

Standing in the doorway, was Sergeant Goodwin. He'd arrived earlier than expected and for a few seconds he said nothing. He then spoke slowly and deliberately,

"What-on-earth, are you two doing up to dressed like that?" He added, " This is intolerable ... I was warned about you by the Sengo and I'm afraid I'll have to ring him and inform him of this immediately."

Ben flipped up his visor and glanced in Dixie's direction. They nodded in unison as if they were in telepathic connection to each other, lunging at Sergeant Goodwin, they wrestled him to the ground. It was not difficult at all as Goodwin was only five foot four inches tall and couldn't have been more than nine stone in weight.

Dixie held their captive firmly pinned down, while Ben ran off to find something suitable with which to tie him up with. What he came back with was a large canvas mail sack and a roll of strong sticky tape. With very little difficulty, they bundled the poor helpless, admin sergeant into the sack and sealed the neck using several feet of the sticky tape. Sergeant Goodwin emitted pitiful yells of protest, which were effectively muffled by the thick, strong canvas material. Ben dragged the sack along the polished floor and into a small cupboard, which contained the mops, brushes and other cleaning equipment. He locked the door and threw the key into a nearby waste-paper bin.

Walking into the crew room, he found Dixie who was calmly making a couple of mugs of coffee. A kitbag, which contained their civilian clothes, had been collected by Dixie from his locker and was stood on one of the tables nearby. Dixie smiled and spoke:

"Well, Benny Boy, there's no going back now is there? Whatever else we do, we're up for a court martial at the very least." Ben reached for his mug, nodding in agreement and after sipping at the scalding hot coffee, he replied,

" You're right, Dixie. I suppose we had better get the show on the road."

Together, they returned to the flying clothing section to collect the kit they needed. As they passed by the locked cupboard, they both heard but did not acknowledge the muted shouts of Sergeant Goodwin from within. They swiftly removed their flying suit, removed their uniform from underneath and each put on a pair of jeans and a sweatshirt. Before they donned the flying suits and jackets again, they fitted the bulging money-belts around their waists. After collecting their helmets from the storage rack, both headed out to the HAS.

As they were about to leave the building via the flight line control, the telephone rang. Instinctively, Ben picked it up and answered with his rank and name as he'd done innumerable times before. Ben swore under his breath, when he realized he should have just ignored the phone. The voice on the other end was very familiar. It was Sengo Burton and he spoke:

"Good Morning, Corporal Brownley, I need to speak to Sergeant Goodwin. Could you get him to the phone? "

Ben cupped the mouthpiece in his hand and he whispered to Dixie saying,

" It's Burton on the phone. He wants to speak to Goodwin. What should I say? "

Dixie's face erupted into a smile and Ben knew he was about to utter some stupid comment,

"Tell Burton we've given him the sack, so he can't come to the phone," replied Dixie. Ben shook his head and whispered as loud as he dared:

"Stop pissing about Dixie. What should I say?"

Dixie stroked his chin as if he was trying to make out he was in deep contemplation. This time he replied,

" Tell him that the Sarge is on the bog and he'll ring him back. Now let's go, because we're late for an appointment with our destiny" he added mockingly. Ben relayed the advice to Sengo Burton in an unaccustomed abrupt manner and quickly replaced the receiver. He had to run to catch up with Dixie who had walked on ahead and was already near the entrance of the HAS.

As soon as they entered the HAS, they busied themselves with the final preparation for boarding the aircraft and starting the engines. Dixie jumped into the cockpit and started the auxiliary power unit. It provided the vital, 115 volts of AC electrical power. There was over fourteen miles of electrical wiring that filled every available nook and cranny of the aircraft's structure. Instantly, the wires pulsed with the signals and data that fed into the multitude of computers, actuators and switches and it also enabled him to run-up the navigation kit and loaded the mission route into the on-board computer. Ben walked around the outside of the aircraft, removing all the safety pins from the undercarriage ground locking devices and of course, from the two weapons hanging beneath the fuselage. He produced a small piece of white chalk from his pocket; he wrote on the nose of the right hand bomb, ' Wally's Revenge." As a gesture and he was sure that he had seen it on some old war movie somewhere.... he patted the bomb for luck. His final task was to kick the chocks clear of the wheels. The normal crew ladder was not fitted, so he climbed onto the external fuel tank, up on to the wing and into the front cockpit.

Ben removed the ejection seat safety pins and strapped himself into the seat and parachute. He carefully connected his oxygen hose and intercom lead so he could speak to Dixie who was already strapped into the ejection seat in the back cockpit and had all the avionics kit ready and he awaited engine start-up. Ben closed the canopy, which lowered slowly to the deafening blare of a warning horn, and checked it was firmly locked. This distinctive audible signal could often be heard all over the site and most of the station. Ben was concerned that this may betray their presence on the site and draw premature attention to their illegal intentions. But it was too late to worry about it at that stage, so Ben pressed on.

He quickly ran through the checks and started up both engines, as he had countless times before during engine ground testing. Powering up the aircraft flying control systems, as he had done in the simulator throughout the past months, came as a natural function to him. Ben thought to himself, that he felt as if he had be doing the cockpit drills for years.

With the aircraft ready to roll, all Ben had to do was to release the parking brake and the Alpha Lima would escape the confines of the HAS and move out into the unusually brilliant sunshine, that beat down on that September morning. Ben reached for the brake with his right hand, but before he released it, he spoke to Dixie:

" This is it, Dixie... your last call to pull out. What will it be?"
Dixie replied,

"Go for it, Benny Boy, go for it! Those delegates will be streaming towards the conference centre on Llandudno pier by now and we have a package to deliver."

Ben released the parking brake and inched the twin throttles slightly forward. Alpha Lima advanced and thirty ton of man, machine and weapon emerged out of the HAS into the warm early autumn sunlight. Ben had another reason for selecting Alpha Lima, which he hadn't revealed to his pseudo navigator. It was because the HAS, in which Alpha Lima was housed, had almost a straight run to the main taxiway. Many of them had tight right or left hand bends to negotiate on leaving the HAS, of course all real pilots could manoeuver their aircraft, with eminent expertise, in and out of any close confine, Ben wasn't that confident, when steering the aircraft on the ground.

As the aircraft rolled slowly towards the main taxiway, Ben scanned the cockpit instruments and everything seemed to be just right. Glancing into the mirrors mounted on the canopy frame, he adjusted them slightly to get a view of his wing tips, which were both bouncing alarmingly as the aircraft rumbled along the tarmac surface. Ben knew that this was quite usual as he had seen it, from the outside, hundreds of times before, as aircraft trundled past around the dispersal.

Ben was concentrating hard on steering his aircraft slowly but accurately along the narrow taxyway. As he approached the slight turn, which would take him onto the main taxyway, Dixie spoke over the intercom,

" Look left, Benny Boy, I think we have someone to wave us off."

Ben swivelled his head to look over to the left. He saw a Volvo pull up and Squadron Leader Burton stepped out of its drivers-side door. The Sengo stared over towards the Alpha Lima as it headed along the taxyway, which ran alongside of the squadron car park. For a brief moment he did not react to the situation but he then realized that no aircraft should have been operating on that day and definitely should not be attempting to take off. Burton could not understand, who was going flying. Surely, he thought, as the Senior Engineering Officer he should have been informed of any unscheduled flying during a German public holiday. He walked towards the moving aircraft to try and get a better look at who was crewing it.

Inside the cockpit Ben and Dixie had pulled down their dark visor to disguise their features. As Alpha Lima drew closer to Sengo Burton, Ben spoke into the intercom,

" Aircrew salute, Dixie." In unison, they both threw up a 'Top Gun' type naval salute but with their left hand.

Burton was confused. He moved as if he was going to return the salute then changed his mind. Instead he shaded his eyes against the strong sunshine to see if he could identify the crew. Ben spoke again,

" OK Dixie, visors up, masks off and give him a groundcrew salute instead. " Again, with a synchronized movement they raised their visors, unclipped their face-masks and delivered a two-fingered gesture towards Burton.

As soon as Burton recognized the features of the two aircrew, who stared down at him from the cockpit, his own face drained. He started to jog alongside the moving aircraft, waving frantically in a futile attempt to stop its progress towards the runway. He had to break into a run but couldn't keep pace with the aircraft, which by now, had accelerated up to normal taxy speed. Soon, Sengo Burton was running as fast as he could behind Alpha Lima, as it pulled away. Ben could see him in his cockpit mirrors. In a final gesture of insubordination he opened both the throttles to generate a powerful, but brief, blast of thrust from the exhausts of both engines. The movement of such a large volume of hot air, aimed directly at the running figure of Burton, forced him to stagger uncontrollably sideways towards the grass verge of the taxyway. He lost his footing on the grass, tripped over and careered into a large muddy puddle, which had remained following the recent heavy rain. This comical event was both witnessed by Ben and Dixie, via their cockpit mirrors, and they cheered loudly together into their face masks.

Ben soon forgot their pursuer and returned to the task in hand. He steered the aircraft onto the runway and taxied slowly over the arrestor cable and brought the aircraft to a halt in the centre of the wide expanse of concrete that formed the first hundred feet of runway. The black tarmac runway stretched away into the hazy distance. Ben took a deep breath, closed his eyes for a few seconds and prepared himself for the next and final phase of Operation Twickenham.

CHAPTER 14

Ben quickly checked around the cockpit in readiness for take of, ensuring that the slender grey wings were selected forward and the flaps, which greatly enhances the vital lift characteristics the wings produce during the take off run, were selected to half down. This would enable the heavily laden, 30-ton Tornado to get airborne. While he was doing this, Dixie was switching through the various radio channels in an attempt to find the local civil aircraft controller's frequency. He needed to listen in, so he could have some idea what they might find when they finally left terra firma.

Ben stared down the runway through the shimmering haze, which was a produce of the rapidly rising temperature of the black, tarmacadamed surface. He searched for any signs of movement ahead. He knew that when the runway was closed for flying, and even on public holidays, the motorized runway sweeper would be trailing methodically up and down the length and breadth of the runway and taxiways, which was vital to keep the surfaces clear of stones and debris. Should any of these be sucked into the intakes of the engines, they could cause severe damage or even inflict fatal consequences onto the aircraft and its crew. Ben strained his eyes to see ahead but he saw nothing.

Ben advanced both the throttles forward. The engines accelerated rapidly and their gauges spun up to indicate that maximum core engine power was available and their gas temperatures were reading within limits. Casting an expert eye over the engine indications, he moved the throttles further forward and into the afterburner or reheat range, as it was always referred to by the engine tradesmen. He felt a gentle, double thump from the rear of the airframe; this implied that the carefully metered quantity of reheat fuel that had been injected into the titanium jet-pipes had ignited. As soon as the nozzle gauges indicated that 50 % reheat had been achieved on both engines, Ben released the aircraft brakes.

Both the nozzle gauges continued increasing to maximum reheated power as the aircraft rapidly gathered forward momentum. The acceleration seemed slower than he had experienced during his back-seat trip...and this concerned Ben. Suddenly, it dawned on him that Alpha Lima had two under-wing external tanks fitted and, of course, it was also carrying two 1000 pound HE bombs. To counter this, Ben pushed the throttles a few centimeters further forward, with which to engage combat power, which gave for a limited period, both of the powerful RB199 engines, an additional five percent more thrust, thereby restoring the rate of acceleration to a comfortable margin.

Alpha Lima was rocketing down the runway. Its twin reheats crackled and spat flames rearwards with a combined thrust of over thirty-two thousands pounds. The thunderous noise, that was an unwelcome by-product of its paraffin guzzling engines, radiated outward and well beyond the boundaries of the station and into the local sleepy hamlets and villages which surrounding the air base. On his previous flight Ben had naturally felt a considerable adrenaline surge, but to be in total control of the aircraft himself provided an unbounded exhilaration, that was beyond even his own, vivid imagination. Dixie must have been experiencing similar emotions, because he was cheering loudly into his intercom and shouted to Ben for the first time since they had left Burton in their hot, fumey wake,

"This is brilliant, Benny Boy, Go for it!"

Ben was concentrating hard on the job of getting Alpha Lima off the ground. The Tornado powered its way past the ATC tower, which was located on their right hand side of the runway. For some strange reason he found himself reciting into his intercom, some very appropriate words of a song from his favourite pop group - The Moody Blues.

" *Blasting, Billowing, Bursting Forth with the power of ten billion butterfly sneezes,*
Man with his flaming pyre has conquered the wayward breezes,
Climbing to tranquillity, far above the cloud,
Conceiving the heaven, clear of misty shroud. "

Alpha Lima sped down the runway. Ben vaguely registered the two 3000 metre marker boards, which were positioned on each side of the broad runway. He was eagerly awaiting the aircraft to exceed 155 knots, by when, he had expected the aircraft's nose to begin to lift. The additional payload that the Alpha Lima was carrying delayed that point of lift-off perhaps a little longer than Ben had anticipated resulting sweat to run profusely from his body and the flow was only stemmed when all of the aircraft's wheels finally lifted off clear of the runway. A huge sigh of relief emitted from Ben as he confessed to his rear seat partner,

" Bloody hell, Dixie, I thought we'd never get off the deck."

Dixie gleefully replied,

" But you did it, Benny Boy, you did it!"

As soon as they had cleared the airfield boundary, which on the western perimeter was over a mile from the runway threshold, Ben lifted the flaps and undercarriage. The Dutch border was only a short distance beyond that perimeter so Ben, Dixie and their titanium £20 million charger left German airspace... forever.

Ben steadied the aircraft and built up the speed to 350 knots. He pulled back firmly on the control column to aim the aircraft skywards. But Dixie didn't have time to admire the view, as he was head down operating the many systems that fall under the responsibility of the rear seat occupant. The most important task for him was to initiate the on-board electronic counter measures equipment that would, hopefully, confuse any radar that might be monitoring them during their initial climb to height.

Peering through the front windscreen and looking up at the azure blue cloudless sky, Ben called out to Dixie,

" OK, Mr Navigator, now find me an airliner on that magic box of tricks you have back there."

"Yes, Skipper," came Dixie's prompt but mildly sarcastic reply.

Dixie busied himself with the radar kit to methodically search the sky above. The presence of any aircraft would appear as a blip on the small cathode ray screen in the back cockpit. Within a few seconds the intercom sounded in Ben's ears,

" Target spotted, Skipper, its moving right to left at about 27000 feet and it's doing about 320 knots." exclaimed Dixie in a knowledgeable and confident manner.

Ben scanned the segment of sky through the right hand side of the canopy. Alpha Lima was still rapidly increasing in altitude and was passing through 15000 feet when Ben saw a Boeing 747 traversing their current heading its four massive engines each left a thin, transparent contrail, which was only just visible and trailed back a few miles behind. Ben acknowledged to Dixie that he had a visual contact of the target and eased back on the throttle and out of the reheat range to slow the high closing speed between them and the 747. Ben also pushed the stick forward to abate their rate of climb to permit him to manoeuver the Tornado behind and just below the massive airliner.

The distance between each aircraft steadily reduced. Ben soon recognized the distinctive and colourful livery of the British Airways Jumbo Jet, which was ploughing westwards through the thin air. Its crew and three hundred or so fare-paying passengers were oblivious to the presence of the fighter-bomber, which was silently stalking them. Ben had to make several small adjustments of both throttles and flying controls to position Alpha Lima in the precise position that he desired. Their Tornado aircraft was slowly creeping underneath the imposing frame of the Jumbo as Ben steered the aircraft directly under its centre line and about forty feet below it. Of course, he had deliberately planned this method of evasion to camouflage their position. It had come to him as he watched the stream of aircraft fly over their woody glade, both he and Dixie had often rested at, so by using the Jumbo as a shield, it would help to elude any pursuing interceptor aircraft. He was unsure of how long it would take the authorities to react to the theft of the Tornado aircraft but equally he was dead certainly that Sengo Burton would have quickly informed the Station Commander at Feldbruch. But how soon that information could generate a reaction or response, Ben had no idea. Only five minutes had elapsed since Alpha Lima had lifted off German soil. Ben thought to himself, "So far, so good!"

Both of them were looking vertically up through their own section of the canopy at the huge shape that seemed to be floating motionless above. Ben glanced left to right. He looked in awe, at the gigantic wingspan that shielded the invisible rays of the sun. Hanging beneath those wings were the four air-gobbling Rolls Royce RB211 engines, which droned on at a steady monotonous throb and constantly defied gravity to propel the huge airliner into the skies. Ben set Alpha Lima's autopilot at their current altitude and speed. He knew that commercial jets very rarely changed either height or speed once they had attained their designated cruising altitude and he spoke into his face mask mounted microphone to remind Dixie to switch off the counter measure equipment, as it was not necessary during this phase of the flight. He also asked him to scan down with the radar to watch for any approaching aircraft. Dixie swiftly acknowledged this request confirming that he had already activated the on-board, radar homing receiver equipment, which would indicate if any preying eyes of ground-based or airborne radar were looking for them. Ben was confident, however, that being so close to the 747, its huge shape and radar return should mask their presence. At best it would deter any close advance from interceptor aircraft and would certainly stop any attempt at shooting them down. Ben smiled inwardly and contently to himself. This element of Operation Twickenham, that he had devised those many months ago, whilst lying on the grass in the clearing at Feldbruch, seemed to be running to schedule and as planned.

A few minutes later Dixie spoke from the back cockpit,

"Benny Boy, we're just crossing the Dutch coast just south of Amsterdam. On this heading we should break the English coast somewhere near the Humber estuary."

Ben peered over the cockpit sill to the ground below at the thick layer of cloud far beneath obscuring any sight of land or sea, so he turned his attention to the moving map display in front of him. There he could see on the small scale map of Holland, that the centre marker, which indicated Alpha Lima's position, was moving over the coastline and out into the North Sea. Ben settled back to wait for the short transit time to elapse, until they reached UK airspace. He wriggled about as much as the tight fitting, seat harness would allow. The bulky, note-filled money belt that Ben was wearing was not very comfortable, when sat in the tight confines of the cockpit.

Dixie diverted Ben's attention as he broke in over the intercom,

" Benny Boy, the kit back here is picking up several ground-based radars that are looking at us. I would expect that they would be tracking any aircraft flying over this area, so we needn't worry, as they'll only see the 747 anyway. " Dixie then added, " The good news is, that it doesn't look like any airborne radar's are tracking us...yet!"

Alpha Lima was soon cruising steadily only fifteen miles off the Norfolk coast. The cloud had thinned out and Ben could visually identify the coastline, which matched the image and over-laid radar picture, that was presented on his moving map display screen. Ben thought to himself that it soon would be time to leave the cozy protection of the 'mother hen' Jumbo. A few moments later he disengaged the autopilot and spoke on the intercom to Dixie:

" We're going for the descent. Switch on the counter measure kit again and I'll need a heading from you, when we get down to low level, so we can hit the coast near Skegness." Dixie replied:

" You'll have it, Benny Boy, ...I mean, Skipper."

At first Ben pulled away slowly from the 747's protective shield, then he took their aircraft into a steep but wide spiralling dive. The altimeter swiftly wound down and eventually it levelled off at 1500 feet above the sea. Ben had swung the nose of the aircraft to point towards land, just as Dixie called for a heading of 260 degrees and it only needed a slight rudder adjustment to comply with Dixie's instructions and Ben dropped their altitude down to 250 feet. Half a mile before land break, he jettisoned, into the sea, the now empty external fuel tanks. Despite these tanks being streamline, they did dramatically increase the aerodynamic drag of the aircraft and by unburdening these external appendages from the wings made the aircraft leap forward with a welcomed, newfound thrust. The feel and handling of the aircraft also was far more responsive, which Ben found extremely exciting. He could see the host of brightly coloured caravans, which adorned much of the shoreline, fields and grassed areas around Skegness. They flashed passed in a technicolour blur. The peaceful tranquillity of the thousands of holiday makers were shattered as Alpha Lima thundered overhead causing dogs to bark uncontrollably and small children to run screaming, in fright, to their mothers.

They were fast approaching their first way-point. It was to be RAF Hemingsby. Ben selected the wings rearwards to the mid and optimum position for a strike attack and called out to Dixie to give him a compassing heading, which would allow him to fly straight down the main runway. Dixie duly obliged and they soon found themselves twenty miles out from Hemingsby at 200 feet and on a target run-in. Ben instructed Dixie that he wanted to drop an unarmed bomb right in front of the Air Traffic Control tower. The rational behind such strange actions was quickly explained by Ben,

" I don't want to harm any of the blue uniformed guys. But by letting them see a weapon land adjacent to the runway, it'll stop them ...for a while anyway, from launching any of their interceptor aircraft after us."

Dixie admitted to Ben over the intercom, that his planning and forethought never ceased to amaze him. Ben responded,

" Its' the six Ps, Dixie, you know...Prior, Planning, Prevents, Piss, Poor, Performance!"

Dixie grunted in acknowledgment into the intercom as he frantically worked at his array of avionics equipment. He needed to ensure the weapon's fuses were disarmed so as to enable Ben to drop the 1000 pounder. This would mean, of course, the bomb wouldn't explode on landing, when Ben pressed the red, weapon release button on the control column. Dixie could hear the local air traffic controller on the radio from Hemingsby, requesting   identification and compliance with their controlling instructions.   He flicked a switch, which silenced the sweet sounding voice of a female, who was transmitting from the tower.

Ben could see the parallel lines of the runway landing lights, away in the distance and the long titanium pitot tube, which was mounted on the tip of the sleek nose radome of Alpha Lima neatly bisected them.   He made a very slight movement of the control column, which moved the line of runway lights to pass just left of his centre.   This was designed to enable the weapon to fall exactly, where Ben wanted it too.   Dixie shook his head in mild astonishment, as he realised that this was yet another example of the small but essential detail of Ben's planning.   He was beginning to comprehend that Ben must have spent hours and hours of time in deep contemplation and planning over Operation Twickenham and a personal feeling of guilt over his small, insignificant contribution towards what was supposed to be, a joint effort.

Alpha Lima crossed the perimeter fence of RAF Hemingsby at 0843 hours UK time at just above 200 feet and travelling at 400 knots.   It streaked over a lone F3 Tornado, which was taxiing on to the eastern threshold of the runway. Ben gave it a quick glance and realized it was armed with at least two Sidewinder heat-seeking missiles and he knew that it represented a major threat to their mission should it get airborne in pursuit of them. But again, his amazing forthought and the minute details he had compiled to cover such an eventuality, his master plan would scotch that threat within a few seconds.

The attacking GR5 powered towards the target's aiming point. A red flare arched up from the ATC tower, which is the standard warning if radio contact with an approaching aircraft could not be gained. Ben ignored it and on Dixie's signal, he pressed the weapon release button and a muffled thump was felt through the airframe, as the twin cartridges in the weapon ejector release mechanism fired. The menacing, dark green shape of a one thousand pound HE bomb left the aircraft. It was punched away from the fuselage by the two powerful pistons, propelled by the cartridge gases and the now disarmed weapon fell away towards the ground.

Several people saw the aircraft approaching and the bomb fall from beneath it. Two young firemen, who were stood outside the ATC tower, witnessed the amazing events. It took them only a few microseconds to react before they dived to the ground in anticipation of the deafening explosion and potential lethal blast that should have followed. Instead, the weapon didn't explode as had been expected.

The unarmed bomb had been dropped below its normal release height, so it crashed into the lushious turf, ploughing a long furrow as it skidded along the soft ground that lay in front of the Air Traffic tower building. Its impact threw up a shower of dirt and soil, which was projected forward and high into the sky almost reaching the height that Alpha Lima was flying at. The brown scar that the weapon exposed in the lush, well kept grass, stretched over twenty feet, before the weight of the bomb forced itself beneath the surface and out of sight.

As soon as Dixie called, " Weapon gone, " Ben slammed the throttles forward to select maximum reheat on both engines and he pulled the wings to the fully back position. Alpha Lima surged forward like a thorough-bread racehorse, as it was suddenly relieved of the weight of one of its under-slung munitions. Ben tried to see the evidence of his action in the cockpit mirrors but a clear view of the ground behind the aircraft, was obstructed by the glare of the flares and clouds of chaff, which Dixie was firing off. These were designed to deflect any heat-seeking or radar guided missiles. None were expected or indeed fired at them but Dixie felt that he needed to make a positive contribution towards their survival and he thought that they'd look impressive anyway.

The Senior Air Traffic Controller immediately suspended flying at Hemingsby and evacuated the immediate area. He was not to know that the bomb was safe and it wouldn't explode at a later time so it was prudent to play safe and await the arrival of the bomb disposal experts. Another piece of Ben's well thought out plan had achieved its desired effect. There would be no fighter aircraft pursuing them from this airfield but Ben knew that it would only be a matter of time, and a short time at that, before armed aircraft would be scrambled from either or both or Hemingsby's sister units in Yorkshire and Scotland.

Alpha Lima thundered over the flat, fertile, Lincolnshire countryside on its way towards Nottingham and the Midlands. Ben had accelerated the aircraft up to 500 knots and at 250 feet it surprised him how smoothly the aircraft flew. Through the windscreen Ben could see a nasty looking weather front approaching. A blackened sky lay straight in front of them. An occasional iridescent flash of lightening lit up the dark backdrop of the clouds, as nature's very own strike attack found its random targets. Dixie was peering over the coning of his cockpit at the approaching weather and registered its potential danger. Such was the size of the black, rain-laden clouds; they even showed up as large green smudge filling the forward quadrant of his radar display. It prompted him to speak to Ben,

" I hope you're not contemplating flying through that lot?"

"Not bloody likely! " replied Ben. He then added, " Wouldn't it be ironic if our mission was terminated by a lightning strike hitting to our aircraft. Us with the squadron markings on the tail fin containing a lightning symbol. So, Dixie, I need a route round or over it, ... and sharpish."

Dixie returned his attentions to his radar display and did not respond for a minute or two. When he did finally speak, it was give Ben the instructions he requested,

" By the looks of the radar picture, Benny Boy, our only option is to go over it because the weather stretches a long way both north and south. Take us up until we clear it but keep on this heading. If we stay on the 53 degree north latitude line, it will take us on to our next way-point."

Ben acknowledged the advice of his navigator and pulled back the stick to take Alpha Lima into a steep climb. At twelve thousand feet they levelled out above the thunder-laden clouds into a beautifully clear sky. But they both knew that they would be highly visible to both ground-based and any airborne radars, which may have been within range. To Dixie's annoyance the counter measures kit, which he had reselected on way back over the sea was beginning to play up and was not functioning as it should. The presence of a flashing amber warning light indicated that a malfunction somewhere within its maze of wires and plethora of circuit boards, diodes and resistors and its effectiveness to hide from preying eyes therefore highly suspect. Almost immediately Dixie picked up the signal that an airborne early warning aircraft, possibly an E3 Sentry, was tracking them. Both Ben and Dixie worked overtime, scanning every quadrant of their field of view to watch for any incoming fighter aircraft. Ben knew that if it came to an aerial fight, they would have no realistic chance of surviving.

Dixie was switching through the radio frequencies to try and pick up any information that might help them. The airwaves were very active but there had been no broadcast, in clear speech, declaring that a rogue RAF Tornado aircraft was flitting around dropping the occasional high explosive bomb here and there. However Dixie picked up one transmission that advised of a military aircraft, which was flying on an unauthorized flight plan.

Alpha Lima headed west and was soon flying over the outskirts of the Cheshire town of Crewe, where the cloud began to quickly thin out. Ben immediately took the aircraft back down to 250 feet in an attempt to evade the E3 Sentry, which had been tracking them for the past ten minutes. Dixie then spoke into his intercom,

" OK, Benny Boy, due to this inclement weather, we've slipped off course slightly. Our next way-point will have to be the Bangor-on-Dee Racecourse, which should be visible just ahead slightly left of centre. When we over fly it, you'll need to turn onto a heading of 322 degrees. That will take us onto our next way-point which will be your Wally's Steelworks at Brymbo."

Ben looked through his left hand quarter-light windscreen and there in front was the unmistakable shape of the horse racing course, which he had seen many time on the t.v. He told Dixie that he had a visual on the racetrack. Then, as instructed, he changed course onto 322 degrees, as the spectators grandstand disappeared beneath their aircraft. Alpha Lima surged onwards - on its mission of revenge.

Ben readjusted the speed to 350 knots. With the Esclusham Mountains approaching he steadily raised the altitude to clear the ground below by a hundred and fifty feet or so. Below the right hand side of the aircraft lay his home town of Wrexham. Ben recognized many of its features and landmarks. Some, but not all, looked different from 350 feet up. The football ground was a very familiar sight and he could just make out that several players were training on the pitch. To the east of the large colourful football stand, Ben could also see the pitch and small clubhouse, where he had first played rugby many years previous.

Ben's attention then returned to the view through the front windscreen. He could see the painted white building complex that was his own school many years ago. However it was the sight of the Steelworks, or what was left of it that really stirred his nostalgic emotions. He was aware that the huge works had been almost completely demolished. But it wasn't until he saw the magnitude of the vast site from the air, which had been converted into a huge derelict wasteland, that he fully understood why Wally felt so strongly about its demise. Ben banked the aircraft over to the right, as it flew over the remains of the steel-rolling mill, where Wally had once worked. A small tear formed in Ben's eye as they left the works site behind and flew very near to the crematorium, where Wally's remains had been laid to rest.

Dixie broke abruptly into Ben's thoughts by speaking into his intercom,

"Ben there is an aircraft crossing our heading about five miles ahead. I don't know what it is, as he's not transmitting his radar. He could be heading for the low level training area to the west."

Ben acknowledged Dixie's observation but he couldn't make a visual identification of the aircraft.

A few moments later Dixie broke in again with a change of course. He explained:

" Sorry, Ben, a slight miscalculation. When we get to that large t.v. mast up ahead, turn onto a heading of 294 degrees. That will take us over the town of Abergele. From there we need to fly out over the sea for five miles and, when we are directly opposite Rhos Point, you can make the final turn onto 270 degrees for the target run-in." Ben quickly confirmed that he had noted the instruction from Dixie as he readjusted the fuel in the tanks to trim the aircraft's balance. Ben peered through the windscreen for the sight of the tall, Harlech TV mast towering high above the mountain summit, which itself, was over fifteen hundred feet high. As it passed on the left of the Alpha Lima, Ben pushed slightly on the rudder peddle to alter their heading onto 294 degrees and readjust his altitude slightly to keep a constant hundred feet or so above the green and purple, heather-covered hillside. He knew this part of the countryside well and was trying to spot places on the ground that he could recognize. Suddenly Dixie spoke anxiously into the intercom,

" Benny Boy I don't want to alarm you but that E3 Sentry's up above and over to the east of us. It's still tracking us and the radio traffic is buzzing. According to the radio chat there's a couple of F3's coming down from the north and another pair are being steered in our direction from the east. We could be in deep shit here, Ben. I think we should turn west, skip the target and head over to Snowdonia and bang out as planned." Ben replied abruptly,

" No! - We haven't come this far not to complete the mission. We'll press on... They can't stop us, we're nearly there." Dixie mumbled unintelligibly into his intercom. He wasn't all that happy with the prospects of being shot at. And he was sure that was becoming more than a distinct possibility.

Alpha Lima powered its way just above the hilltops along the route so meticulously planned by Dixie. Ben strained his eyes to get any glimpse of incoming fighter aircraft from the skies that stretched away to the north and east. His head swivelled around the cockpit. The helmet he wore was beginning to feel like a ton weight. Even his neck muscles, toned from years of rugby, were beginning to experience fatigue from the 'g' forces placed upon them.

Ben was sweating profusely and concentrating so hard on flying Alpha Lima, that he didn't notice the arrival of another aircraft just off his left hand wing tip. He caught a glimpse of movement out of his peripheral vision and turned his head to look. Shocked at what he saw, he physically shook at the sight of a GR7 Harrier aircraft that had silently formatted on the left-hand wing tip of their Tornado. Alpha Lima wobbled about uncontrollably for a few seconds, as Ben's right hand reacted with an involuntary jerk at the sight of an unexpected visitor. Dixie snapped up his head from studying his radar displays and shouted to his pilot, as his ill fitting helmet slipped over his eyebrows slightly,

" What the bloody hell's going on, Ben. Are you trying to kill us? " As he called out, he also spotted the newly-arrived wing man. Dixie spoke again this time in a very alarmed tone as he pushed back his helmet out of his line of vision,

" How the hell did he get there without us seeing him?"

Ben was calm now and suggested that it was probably the aircraft they had spotted earlier on, which had crossed their heading. A Harrier, which had no radar, would not show up on the avionics equipment, when approaching from the rear of their aircraft. Ben added that with his attention focused on the forward sphere of view, he admitted that he hadn't been monitoring his mirrors. The Harrier would have had an easy job formatting on their aircraft.

Ben climbed the aircraft slightly to get a good look at the Harrier. It was a twin-stick, trainer version. To Ben's extreme relief, he noted that it was not armed with any air-to-air missiles and was in the process of weighing up his options, when the Harrier rear seat crewman raised a white card with the words, 'Follow Me' written on it. He beckoned over to Ben with his hand and gave a thumb's up gesture. There was no radio contact from Alpha Lima as Ben had previously decided that no transmissions would be made, to anyone. The Harrier crew had been trying, in vain, to raise a response from Alpha Lima's crew. It left the Harrier crew with hand signals as the only means of communication. Ben nodded in agreement to the Harrier crew and waggled the wings of his Tornado in response. The Harrier pulled up slightly and started to turn slowly to the left.

Dixie hung his head in defeat, his ill-fitting helmet slipped forward over his eyebrows yet again. He knew that Ben had made the right decision and thought to himself, that the Harrier must have been vectored onto them by a military air traffic controller in a attempt to try and persuade them to head back to the nearest military airfield. Dixie could now see that the game was up. He resigned himself to accepting whatever punishment the Air Force would meter out for misappropriating a military fighter and a couple of HE bombs.

Suddenly, Ben slammed both throttles to maximum reheat and then into combat power and the Tornado shot forward like an arrow from a bow and it left the slower Harrier in its turbulent wake. Dixie was forced back into his seat and, as he pushed back his helmet out of his line of sight, he yelled into his intercom,

" Jesus Christ! Ben, what the hell are you doing? "
Ben replied in annoyance, " The mission that we set out to do in the first place, of course. So do your soddin' job and arm the friggin' weapon, I reckon we've only twenty miles to go."

Dixie was now very agitated. He shouted into his intercom, as his breathing became fast and loud, "But Ben, there's four incoming fighters, who are not going to be so easy to slip away from. For god's sake, let's get out of here."

Ben repeated, more calmly this time, his request for the weapon to be armed in readiness to drop. Dixie could see he was not going to dissuade his pilot from completing the mission. Reluctantly he started to go through the arming sequence, as Ben continued to scan the skies for any potential threat. Every second that passed brought Alpha Lima closer to the target and to the act of violent revenge. To begin with the whole idea had been seen by Dixie as a bit of lark and a direct challenge to the authority of the Air Force, now it was very real, extremely imminent and worrying Dixie, shitless.

The shoreline of the small seaside town of Abergele slipped by a thousand feet below the speeding form of Alpha Lima. Now the reality of what Ben was about to commit really hit home to Dixie and it scared him so much that his hands were shaking and he had difficulty making the correct switch selections to arm and drop the weapon.

Dixie finally completed the task and returned to the radar display to try and locate the F3 aircraft, which were racing in for an unwelcome rendezvous with Alpha Lima and its crew. Two blips appeared on Dixie's radar display. They were the F3s and they were only fifty miles to the north of their position and closing on them rapidly. Dixie also picked up another contact, which was a low flying, slow moving aircraft approximately seven or eight miles off Rhos Point. Ben gripped tightly on the control stick and steered out to sea and towards the next and final turning point. Dixie saw the distinctive bright yellow pain work of a Search and Rescue helicopter away in the distance. It was hovering close to the sea's surface and he could just make out the shape of a vessel close by. They were probably practicing winching drills or perhaps it could have been for real, Ben thought to himself.

Dixie had heard nothing from Ben for several seconds. But the radio waves were alive with chattering conversations and instructions, which related, mostly, to the ongoing operation with the 'off course' military aircraft. The signs didn't look at all good. Dixie quickly glanced at the fuel gauge readout. The contents remaining in the tanks were low and dwindling fast and he was concerned that they wouldn't have sufficient fuel to make Capel Curig, where they intended to part company with Alpha Lima.

As if by telepathy Ben must have sensed Dixie's' concern over the fuel state. He de-selected reheat on both engines to slow their speed slightly in preparation for the attack, but also to help conserve fuel. Dixie spoke to Ben again but by now his voice couldn't disguise his fear for their imminent future.

" Ben, For God's sake, lets get out of here. We can get back at the TUC some other way ...head south for Snowdonia and..."

Ben snapped back at his best mate,

" Shut up, Dixie. Shut up. I need your help to finish the job off. I'm not going to stop now ...we're nearly there."

Alpha Lima continued over the sea and t he distinctive crescent-shaped Bay of Colwyn could clearly be seen off the left wing tip. It ran from Old Colwyn, through the larger seaside town of Colwyn Bay then on to Rhos-on-Sea. Just as Dixie had stated, at five miles out Rhos Point lay direct to the left of their aircraft. Ben pushed hard on the rudder pedals and eased the stick over to the left to bring the nose of the aircraft onto a heading of 270 degrees. This change of course took the oncoming F3's out of the radar's search quadrant and left Dixie blind to their position. Alpha Lima was flying at 900 feet above the sea at 400 knots and was going into a shallow dive to bring the aircraft at 250 feet above the target at the weapon release point.

Dixie was monitoring the radio transmissions. He'd picked up one, which was directed straight at them. It was most probably from the E3 Sentry aircraft calling for the crew of Alpha Lima to respond immediately. When the E3 aircraft received no answer, it sent a further message a few minutes later, which sent a chill down Dixie's spine. It confirmed that there were armed F3 aircraft on-route to intercept their Tornado GR5 and any aggressive or evasive action would be met by an appropriate response. To Dixie that only meant one thing. They would shoot Alpha Lima down if necessary and certainly if they saw them attack the Conference Centre.

Ben had ignored the radio chatter and was breathing hard into his face mask. The noise was being transferred, via the intercom, into Dixie's ears and it drowned out the sound of his navigator's renewed plea to pull out of the attack. The thought of killing hundreds of people, many of whom were completely innocent of Wally's death, troubled Dixie. He knew that revenge of this magnitude was clearly wrong.... whatever the provocation.

Alpha Lima was only 4 miles from the Conference Centre. The target nestled at the foot of the huge Great Orme Mountain, which dominated the seaside town of Llandudno. The resort's wide shingle beach spread eastwards from where the Grand Hotel's Conference Centre stood. The eastern extremity of the bay was marked by the rocky outcrop, which was the Little Orme Mountain. It was four hundred and twenty feet high and lay in direct line of sight with Alpha Lima and the target aiming point. Ben would have to fly directly over the Little Orme with only forty or fifty feet to spare to enable the precise attack profile to be carried out.

Alpha Lima moved to within 3 miles of the target, when Dixie finally realised what his conscience had been screaming at him for the past twenty miles. He had to act and act fast to stop Ben committing genocide. He knew he had no direct control over the aircraft but he racked his brain for a solution. Scanning the vast array of gauges, switches and dials in his cockpit, he looked for some way to put a stop to the unfolding madness of Operation Twickenham.

Dixie suddenly saw the answer on the left hand side control panel. His index finger pushed the vivid red button, which would jettison all weapons from the pylons beneath the wings and fuselage. A muffled thump was all that was felt as the last remaining thousand pound bomb was pushed clear of the aircraft's fuselage.

At first Ben did not register the firing of the cartridges that released the weapon. But as the aircraft was relieved of its remaining heavy burden, it suddenly rose in altitude. Ben instinctively countered the unexpected climb with a swift nudge forward with the control column to return the aircraft back to the same dive profile. Ben's skills as a pilot were growing by the minute. It unfortunately resulted in a chain of events that brought the doomed aircraft to a sudden and terminal demise. His quick reactions had ensured Alpha Lima had maintained its steady dive profile and only cleared the Little Orme by the required forty feet or so.

The 1000-pound bomb, which was rendered by the electrical circuitry of the jettison system, fell from the aircraft and like the bomb dropped at Hemingsby was not primed to explode on impact. The bomb had only travelled a short distance vertically down when it collided with the rocky hilltop of the Little Orme Mountain at the precise moment the Alpha Lima was skimming close over its summit. The impact of the 1000 pounder striking solid rock at just less than 400 mph caused the iron casing of the weapon to shatter into dozens of fragments. The steel nose-cap of the bomb, released from its tight attachment, ricocheted like a bullet, up and forwards. It was closely followed by a multitude of steel shrapnel shards and lumps of rock.

The shower of metal and rock debris clattered into the rear fuselage of Alpha Lima, as it passed over the Little Orme less than forty feet above its' summit. Most of the smaller rock fragments bounced off or just dented the titanium skin of the aircraft but some of the larger pieces penetrated the aluminum panels that shrouded the rudder and fin of the Tornado. Beneath these panels, ran numerous hydraulic pipes and electrical cables, which were easily severed by the sharp rock pieces. Hydraulic oil immediately started spewing out of the rear of the aircraft and the electrical wires, which had been cut, instantly ceased to supply the vital alternating current that powered a multitude of systems of the aircraft. However it was the larger, deadly steel fragments of the bomb casing that punctured any part of the airframe that it came into contact with. They shattered pipes, cables and any components they encountered. Unfortunately it was the steel nose cone of the weapon that had the most devastating effect on Alpha Lima when it careered into the rear fuselage, it sliced into the panel like a hot knife through butter. The first component it impacted was one of the two, taileron flying control, hydraulic actuators, completely severing its stainless steel ram and cutting through a bundle of cables that carried the vital signals from the fly-by wire compute.

The lethal, nose cone was then deflected, following its contact with the actuator to continue on its destructive path. The fly-by wire systems of the Tornado had a last ditch mechanical back up consisting of a single metal rod that connected the pilots control column with the taileron. This gave a rudimentary flying control system in the event of total automatic system failure. The ricocheting nose cone swiftly severed that rod, leaving Ben with no ability to control either the altitude or the attitude of the aircraft. The control column soon was left feeling like a limp, impotent dick in his hand.

Startled by the multiple impacts from the back of the fuselage, it was Ben's first indication that something was wrong. The damage inflicted by the fragmented bomb casing and rocks caused a devastating catalogue of events that, in an instant, signalled the end of Operation Twickenham.

Ben's cockpit panels instantly lit up like a Christmas tree, as system after system failed, warning horns sounded and lights flashed. Struggling to regain control of the aircraft, Ben wrestled in vain with the useless control column. He shouted into his intercom, to Dixie,

" Dixie, Dixie, I can't control it!"

Dixie had also felt the multiple impacts to aircraft. He loosened his harness to enable him to twist round in his seat to try and see what was happening at the rear of the aircraft. He could see the hydraulic fluid spraying out, which was quickly atomized by the fierce slipstream.

Alpha Lima was still diving steadily towards the target, which was only a mile and a half away. The Tornado's huge taileron flying control surface was left unpowered and uncontrolled in the slipstream. The taileron pitched nose down slightly under its own weight and the aircraft started to roll slowly over to the right and Ben was powerless to stop it. He realized that if the aircraft rolled completely over, that neither of them would be able to eject. The sea was less than two hundred feet below. Ben screamed into his intercom,

" Eject, Eject." He then added in utter panic, " Get out, Dixie, for Christ's sake, get out. She's going over! "

Dixie froze for a moment. He then made a frantic grab, with both hands, at the yellow and black ejection seat firing handle positioned between his legs. He yanked the handle up and waited for the seat to fire. It only took an instant for the canopy rocket motors to ignite and catapult the 2 cwt of canopy, clear of the doomed Tornado. A multitude of complex safety devices, which were ingeniously designed by the Martin Baker Company, who had built and supplied ejection seats for the Royal Air Force since they were introduced in the late 40s, took less than a third of a second to initiate the firing of the seat.

The ejection seat travelled up the guide rail and massive 'g' forces were exerted onto Dixie's body. He had loosened his harness a few moments earlier to look to the rear of the aircraft but that instinctive action was never corrected. To prevent injury, it was absolutely essential that the correct posture was adopted for ejection. The 'g' forces acting on Dixie's body, allowed his upper torso to move forward a few inches and away from the backrest of the seat, his head and loose fitting helmet was rapidly forced down causing his chin to thump hard into his breast bone.

As the seat cleared the cockpit, the rocket motor fired from beneath the seat pan. It was designed to boost Dixie and the seat up to a safe height for the parachute to open. Dixie had already blacked out under the 'g' forces that resulted in his body's rapid acceleration. As a vicious slipstream of over 390 knots hit him, his body was rammed back into the seat and his head was whipped violently back against the headrest. The slipstream then caught underneath the visor of his ill-fitting helmet, jerking Dixie's head back again and the chinstrap tightened like a vice across his windpipe. The snap of his neck bone was swift and happened within half a second of him pulling the handle. The still unconscious body of Dixie Dean felt no pain. He died instantly.

As soon as the seat reached the zenith of its trajectory, the automatic release mechanism allowed the seat to fall clear and parachute sequencing to deploy the nylon multi-coloured canopy. Dixie floated gently down to the sea, drifted along by the strong southerly winds; he splashed into the water over half a mile to the north of the Little Orme Mountain. He was dead well before he hit the water. His neck was broken by the flying helmet, which he had selected in haste, but had not been fitted correctly.

Alpha Lima continued its agonizingly slow inversion. Ben was soon hanging upside down in his seat straps and being buffeted by the noisy slipstream now the canopy had been dispatched to a water fate. He could see the waves below him, as he was heading inexorable towards the Victorian facade of the Grand Hotel. Ben could clearly see through the front windscreen, the large sign that was mounted above the entrance. Despite being upside down, he could still easily read the words, 'Trades Union Conference 2000'. But out of the corner of his right eye Ben could see a myriad of flashing blue lights. He took a quick glance. He thought he could see a whole cavalcade of police cars, fire engines and ambulances. But then he though that he must have imagined it. Ben swiftly forgot the activities on the promenade and realizing that he had two options. He could either eject, or remain in 'Kamikaze' fashion inside the aircraft and crash into the target. Either way Ben was dead or in dead trouble. He reached for the yellow and black handle between his legs... but he hesitated for a second.

Alpha Lima's profile was like a delta shaped dart, it's two-foot long pitot tube, which extended out in front of the radome, was lined up to pierce the large sign over the hotel's front entrance. Ben pressed the radio transmit button on the stick for the first and only time on the flight. He screamed into his microphone,

"REVENGE!"

That final, dying word was picked up by the orbiting E3 Sentry aircraft. It also watched as the blip on their radar display suddenly disappeared. Alpha Lima's airframe crashed inverted through the ornate front facade of the Grand Hotel. Within a few seconds the famous hotel and Conference Centre was reduced to a pile of crushed bricks, plaster and debris.

Thirty ton of metal colliding at over 400 mph into any building wouldn't leave much standing. The devastating impact of the aircraft crashing into and out through the rear of the hotel, sucked in both the sidewalls. Alpha Lima's progress was instantly stopped as it encountered the solid rock base of the Great Orme, which started its climb at the rear of the hotel. Within a split second of the aircraft hitting the solid limestone monolith, most of complex structure of the aircraft and hundreds of its components had been smashed into tiny, unrecognizable fragments. There wasn't much fuel left in Alpha Lima's tanks but there was enough to generate a deafening explosion and ferocious fire. It melted or distorted everything that remained of the Tornado aircraft. There was nothing left of Ben, except for a few minute bone fragments. Ben had died instantaneously, not knowing about the fate of his long-time mate, Dixie. He had however, gone down fighting. Ben gave his own life in a final act of revenge over the death of his brother, Wally.

CHAPTER 15

An earth shattering explosion echoed along the small peninsular, where the seaside resort of Llandudno lay. Warbling alarms radiated from many of the cars that were parked nearby and flocks of seagulls rose, squawking into the air as the thunderous roar of the explosion rolled over the town. The dust and debris from the Grand Hotel rained down on the promenade and pier within seconds of Alpha Lima's devastating crash. A fleet of fire appliances rushed up to the crash site. They didn't have to travel far. As Ben had seen in his last seconds of his life, they were parked in readiness along the promenade. Ambulances and Police cars joined the fire fighters as they too were in the close proximity of the Grand Hotel. Within a few minutes a Royal Logistics Corps bomb disposal vehicle arrived on the scene. It had reacted to a priority call at 9:00 am to attend the Grand Hotel immediately.

Two F3 Tornadoes roared overhead a few minutes after Alpha Lima terminated its final flight. They circled Llandudno bay twice then they flew off in an easterly direction following their recall to base. It didn't take long for the ten strong fire appliances to bring the fire under control. The limited quantity of fuel, which remained in Alpha Lima, was soon burnt off. The collapsed masonry of the large robust Victorian building had engulfed most of the flammable material and snuffed out the burning contents inside the hotel, as it had fallen with a deafening crash.

Hundreds of people saw the final throws of the Tornado, as it plunged into the building, which they had been occupying less than ten minutes before. The vast majority of the onlookers had the TUC Conference Security Passes pinned onto their chests. Some were physically sick once they realized that they'd all had a very close encounter with the Grim Reaper. If it had not been for the Police's swift action, forcing everyone to evacuate the building due to the bomb threat, each one of them plus the entire staff of the Grand would be underneath the huge pile of bricks and debris that was all that remained of the hotel and conference centre.

The police, now in considerable numbers, rapidly set a cordon around the incident. A large BBC outside broadcast trailer was parked just outside the line of yellow tape that marked the start of the no-go area. Most of the large, expensive, hi-tech TV cameras, which were there to record the conference, had been smashed into unrecognizable pieces beneath the debris of the hotel. A sole cameraman was standing on the top of the trailer with a hand-held video camera. He was trying to capture as much of the aftermath as possible for his scoop-hungry director. He panned along the fire crews, as they searched through the rubble of the Grand Hotel. The camera lens then focused on the shocked faces of the TUC delegates looking for any well-known face of the TUC hierarchy. Suddenly the cameraman swung his lens over to the direction of a Search and Rescue Helicopter, which had just appeared off shore. It hovered half a mile off the Little Orme's headland. A helicopter winchman was lowered into the sea and was quickly hoisted back on board. He took with him a figure he had pulled from the sea. The director shouted up at the cameraman to zoom in and see if he could get a better picture of the rescue. It was impossible to tell whom the figure was or if it was alive or dead. The imposing shape of the large, yellow helicopter, climbed and flew noisily away in a westerly direction beyond the Great Orme.

Within twenty minutes a baying pack of journalists had descended upon the promenade. They had all rushed from their hotels. The reporters had been enjoying a leisurely breakfast before the TUC Conference was due to start its considerable agenda. Up to only a few minutes previously most of them were in no hurry to travel the short distance to the Conference Centre. They all knew that there wouldn't be any newsworthy stories until the speeches and debates started. The main speakers weren't scheduled to begin in earnest until later on that morning.

The massive blast, which came from the direction of the promenade area, prompted a cavalry charge towards the Conference Centre. The reporters feared a terrorist attack. So with notebooks and cameras at hand they raced to the sea front.

When they arrived, they all saw the devastation that had been rendered upon the Hotel and Conference Centre. Reporters and photographers rapidly circulated through the delegates and eyewitnesses. In their usual insensitive and prying manner they asked all sorts of inane questions and even obliquely suggested to their interviewees, 'good newsworthy' words or phrases, that they might wish to offer to the questions they posed.

The posse of pressmen had grown alarmingly. In response and within an hour of the crash, a press conference had been rapidly set up by the Chief Constable of the North

Wales Police Force. A line of tables had been set against the backdrop of the police incident caravan. The Chief Constable sat in the middle and on one side he was joined by the Fire Chief and on the other sat a Royal Air Force Squadron Leader.

A RAF, Sea King helicopter had dropped off Squadron Leader James Lord a few minutes earlier. He had been sent by the MoD to act as the Air Force Liaison Officer and advise the Emergency services.

The Chief Constable spoke first. He confirmed that, despite the horrific crash, there had been no reported fatalities or injuries and added that the area was now safe from explosions, as the aircraft had been confirmed as not carrying any weapons. The journalist fired questions at the three spokesmen. Most of the questions were fielded by the Chief Constable. Inevitably the probing questions of the pressmen lead to the suspected cause of the crash. Squadron Leader Lord took the lead on these questions. He confirmed that the Royal Air Force would of course be setting up a Board of Inquiry immediately. He stated that it would be presumptuous to give any suggestions as to the cause of the crash, before the full facts were known. But the journalists pushed hard for some initial ideas. They even suggested, as they often do, some ludicrous reasons for the crash that they'd dreamt up themselves. It was in an attempt to just goad Squadron Leader Lord into giving some hints, as to what might or might not have caused the loss of the aircraft.

Eventually the hard-pressed officer did offer a crumb of a suggestion that may have caused the accident. He confirmed that the aircraft was on a ferry flight with, unusually for a Tornado, only one crew on-board. He added, that a 'Mayday' call had been received from the aircraft. It had reported that it had hit several large seabirds, whilst flying low over the sea near to the Llandudno area. The Search and Rescue Helicopter, which, purely by chance, was operating within a few miles of the area was quickly dispatched to pick up the pilot from the sea. Before Squadron Leader Lord had finished speaking, a young female reporter near the front of the press audience interrupted and asked the question, which most of the journalists were about to offer:

" Squadron Leader Lord, can you confirm the pilot's name and if he his alive? "
Squadron Leader Lord cleared his throat and replied:

" I'm afraid that standard procedure in the case of a crash is that names would be withheld until the relatives or next of kin are informed. However I am pleased to confirm that the pilot is alive. He was flown to the military medical facility at our base on Anglesey and he has suffered no significant injuries."

Squadron Leader Lord had played his part well. No one suspected that his statement as to the well being of the crew and in fact his version of the whole story was a pack of officially sanctioned lies. The Chief Constable drew the questions to a close but confirmed that a further press conference would be held that evening to bring the media up to date. The press conference then quickly broke up, as the journalists rushed off to register their stories with their editors.

Over in Germany the impact of the treacherous act committed by Corporals Brownley and Dean had already made a mark. Taceval had gone ahead as scheduled because it would have been impossible for it to be postponed without serious questions being asked by NATO HQ. However it had been decided at the highest level within MoD that the full facts regarding the loss of Alpha Lima would be withheld... for the moment at least.

Squadron Leader Burton had been summoned by RAF Feldbruch's Station Commander to a meeting in the Station HQ. Lengthy discussion followed and the events, that led up to the armed aircraft being stolen by two of the squadron groundcrew was analyzed in depth. Jengo Simpson and WO O'Rielly were also interviewed as part of the investigation. Squadron Leader Burton was relieved of his post and ordered back to the Ministry of Defence at Whitehall, London.

Brownley and Dean were immediately posted as AWOL by the Military Police. An officially sanctioned rumour was put out at Feldbruch to explain the absence of the two corporals. It hinted that they had run off to Amsterdam after been found drinking on duty by the Squadron Admin SNCO. To add a bit of drama to the rumour, which was the only true fact of the whole story, the SNCO had been assaulted by the two corporals and locked up in a cupboard.

The official reason why Alpha Lima was not still parked in the HAS was announced by Jengo Simpson. He wasn't happy about the explanation, which he had been told by the Station Commander to release to the ground crew. Nevertheless he confirmed that the aircraft had been recalled back to UK for a special trail fit for a new weapons package. It had come in at extremely short notice, that's why Alpha Lima was flown out on the German public holiday. With Taceval upon the squadron, no one had time to question the information given by the Jengo. Everyone carried on with the exercise and forgot about Alpha Lima, Ben and Dean.

High up on the wind swept side of a mountain near Capel Curig stood the Hafod farmhouse of Mr Percy Brownley. Normally, it would have been unoccupied and secured for the long winter by mid-September. The small windows, which punctuated the thick white-washed walls, emitted a glow of light through the curtains. It showed that someone was in residence. Inside the large downstairs singular room, doubling as a kitchen and sitting room, was Sarah Brownley. She was sat with her feet curled up beneath a large travel rug and was nursing a steaming mug of tea in her hands. A small portable t.v. was perched on an old pine sideboard. Sarah was watching the local evening news bulletin.

The news report was being broadcasted directly from Llandudno. The backdrop of the scene was of the crash site and what was left of the Grand Hotel. Sarah looked on in amazement. She had spent her honeymoon at that hotel many years ago. This was the first time she had heard of the terrible crash, which had happened earlier that day. She heaved a sigh of relief, when she heard the reporter say that no person had been injured. This was mainly due to the bomb threat, which was received at the Conference Centre a few minutes before the crash.

As Sarah watched the news story unfold, the front door opened. In walked a tall figure of a man dressed in a Barbour jacket and Wellingtons. He reached over, kissed Sarah on her head and eased the mug of tea out of her hand.

He took a sip of the scalding hot tea as he kicked off his wellington boots.

Sarah looked over her shoulder at the man that stood behind her. She smiled and spoke to him,

" Hello, Darling. Have you seen what has been going on at Llandudno?" she then added, " Just look at the news on the tele. Isn't it just amazing that no-one was killed or even injured."

Taking off his jacket the man slid onto the couch alongside Sarah. He had long unkempt hair and a full beard. It was a simple but effective disguise from anyone who didn't know him too well. Sarah was sat next to her late husband, Wally Brownley!

They both watched the news together holding hands. The second news conference of the day from the incident control point at Llandudno was being transmitted live. The Chief Inspector chaired the event again. He explained again that they could have been reporting on a very tragic and significant loss of life had the bomb threat not been acted on so swiftly. He confirmed that it was doubtful if it could ever be established, if a bomb had been actually planted or not. The fire and devastation caused by the crash would have destroyed any possible evidence. However, the police would try to seek out the person who had telephoned the bomb threat. The Chief Inspector then gave details of the person they needed to speak to.

" The telephone call came from a public call box in the Snowdonia National Park. He had a local accent and spoke with a noticeable stammer. We would like to speak to this gentleman as soon as possible."

The press conference continued. It repeated that the Ministry of Defence had already set up a Board of Inquiry to investigate the crash and a senior officer would head the official inquiry.

Oblivious to the tragic death of his young brother, Wally looked at his wife and squeezed her hand slightly. Sarah realised that it must have been Wally who'd telephoned the bomb hoax to the Conference Centre She knew it was his way of having a stab back at the TUC for all the awful things they had subjected him to those many months ago. She could also see in his eyes, that he realized his actions had unwittingly saved the lives of all those TUC delegates. If it not been for his hoax call, they would have perished underneath the hotel's Conference Centre.

The final news item on the TV attracted both their attention. The news-caster reported on a missing person's case and said,

" Wrexham Police have scaled down their investigation into the missing Union official, Mr Keith Reece, who had been missing since April. A police spokesman said they had been following a lead, which had now dried up. Mr Reece had been a leading figure in the T&GWU. It had been believed that his disappearance may had been linked to his unpopularity amongst local non-union workers during the industrial action staged in the past year."

Wally watched the news item with a self-satisfied smile on his face and he knew he had succeeded in his violent act of personnel revenge. Wally remembered back to the time five months ago, when he'd bumped into Keith Reece. Wally had met Keith one afternoon while he was walking his dog on the moors behind the site of the Steelworks. His wrath overcame his normally passive nature and he took drastic action on behalf of all those workers, who had suffered at the hands of the union thugs. As a self-appointed judge, jury and executioner he doled out summary punishment. He attacked his one-time friend and knocked him out cold with one powerful punch.

Keith Reece was then tied up and bundled into the back of Wally's car with a blanket thrown over him. Wally, overcome with his passion to seek revenge on his tormentor, then drove down onto the derelict site of his old works. He made a point of letting people see him drive onto the site. He even managed to be seen by the local bobby, as he drove through the gates of the works.

Wally parked up at the back of the old steel rolling mill. It was quiet and deserted and he placed Reece's half unconscious body in the front seat and cut the rope that had bound him. Wally felt no guilt or emotion as he poured a can of petrol over Reece's body and all over the inside of the car. Before he threw a burning box of matches in through the open window, he had to leave evidence for the police to find. He placed his own wedding ring on Reece's finger. Wally then took the St Christopher necklace from around his neck. Sarah had given it to him many years ago on his birthday; it had his initials engraved on the back. He hung it around Reece's neck. Finally Wally placed his penknife into the top pocket of Reece's coat. Wally knew that those items were bound to identify the body as his.

The flames rapidly engulfed the car and within seconds the interior and its occupant were damaged beyond recognition. Wally ran off and slipped inside the old rolling mill shed. He knew the site like the back of his hand, after the many years he had worked there. So he also knew exactly, where to hide until darkness fell.

Within minutes the local police were on the scene, who had been called to the site by the security man after he'd discovered smoke and flames during his rounds. The fire brigade turned up fifteen minutes later. They soon doused down the flames but there wasn't much left of the vehicle or its driver. Keith's body, so badly burnt in the car, had been easily taken for Wally and the personal items he had planted had convinced the police and sadly, Ben as well. Wally, now in his hiding place high in the hills, was contented that Reece had been taken care of and he would never bully or threaten anyone, ever again.

Sarah had tears in her eyes. She knew what Wally had done was illegal and morally wrong. If it ever came out, Wally would be in deep trouble. But just how the police were going to find and arrest a dead man she wasn't certain? Sarah was upset. But what she was really worried about was Ben. She knew she had willingly taken part in the whole charade to make everyone believe that her husband had taken his own life. She asked Wally how they were going to break the news to his brother.

Wally put his arms around his wife and spoke softly to her,

" Ben is due home next month for some leave. You'll have to bring him up here and tell him."
Sarah was shocked when Wally suggested that she would have to tell Ben that the brother he'd grieved for and cremated was in fact, still alive! Wally smiled and explained that it had to be done that way. He knew that if he just

appeared in front of his brother without any warning, it would be too much of a shock for the poor young lad. Wally then told Sarah that he would show himself, after she'd explained to Ben all about their plan to cover up the death of Keith Reece at Wally's hands.

Sarah reluctantly agreed to Wally's idea. She knew the only way to see this tragic situation through was together. But of what the future held she had no idea. They both knew that for the immediate safety they would have to remain in hiding. Wally hugged his wife and kissed her forehead. He was acutely conscious of her very significant part in his act of revenge against Keith Reece. He was also aware of Ben's unintentional role in the whole episode.

Wally squeezed his wife a little tighter and looking into her moist eyes, he said:

" I know that Ben will be shocked, when he hears what I've done. But I know he'll understand. He's not the sort of guy, who could ever hold a grudge against anyone...well not for long. "